DEATH
AT THE
WOOL FAIR

Mrs Capper's Casebook #2

David W Robinson

© David W Robinson 2022

Edited by Maureen Vincent-Northam
Cover Design Rhys Vincent-Northam

No part of this book may be used or reproduced in any manner whatsoever without written permission of the author except for brief quotations used for promotion or in reviews. This is a work of fiction. Names, characters, and incidents are used fictitiously.

Prologue

Good afternoon and welcome to Christine Capper's Comings and Goings, your weekly video blog of what's been happening in Haxford, brought to you by Benny's Bargain Basement. Quality goods at bargain prices, the only place to shop and save.

Now that the case has been resolved in the courts, I can tell you about the awful events at Haxford Wool Fair. It seems such a shame that this long-standing, traditional celebration should be marred by such a terrible incident. I'm not immune to the fun of the fair and I make a point of visiting at least once every year, but this year, my first visit wasn't exactly planned. Instead, it was a phone call on the morning of Thursday, April 21, the day before the fair opened, which drew me into it, and I admit that when I first answered the phone I was deeply suspicious of the caller and his motives.

Chapter One

My vlogs didn't just happen. They needed planning, scripting, rehearsing, then recording, and beyond that they often required careful editing to eliminate interruptions from, say, the postman calling or Cappy the Cat demanding attention.

I usually rehearsed on Wednesday and recorded first thing Thursday morning. By the time I'd done editing, the piece was always ready for posting to my site and the various social media channels I used by Thursday afternoon.

Over the two days of April 20-21, we were blessed with glorious spring sunshine beaming into the back garden. I had made the recording on Wednesday in the conservatory, and on Thursday I was in there again, the back door open, Cappy the Cat basking in the warmth while I got on with the editing. It's a fairly intensive process. I listened through headphones for even the tiniest of distractions, such as a creak from my chair, or the sound of Cappy the Cat rocketing out into the garden because he'd heard the chirp of a squadron of sparrows contemplating a raid on the bird table. I usually picked these noises up while I was recording, and after allowing a short pause, I would repeat whatever passage they had interrupted, so when it came to editing them out, it was a simple process of cutting out the bad passage and using a blend transition, such as a dissolve or fade. If it sounds technical, it isn't. My software had all the necessary facilities and it was more a case of working through the recording and handling those changes.

Even so, it demanded concentration and if there was one thing I did not need, it was an unsolicited phone call, but as Haxford's only licensed private investigator, I had to leave the phone on. So when it warbled for my attention, it was with a good deal of irritation that I made the connection.

"Christine Capper," I announced.

"Am I speaking to Christine Capper?" The voice pronounced my name 'Cappeur' and had a distinct French lilt to it. Either that or he was putting on a poor impression of Hercule Poirot.

"Didn't I just say so?"

"Ah, *oui*. So you did. You are, how you say, a private instigator?"

"Private investigator," I corrected him. "Yes, I am."

"Ah. *Bon*. Could you meet with me, Mademoiselle Capper?"

I tutted. It was one of *those* calls, was it? "For a start off, it's Madame Capper. I'm married, and secondly, I don't meet with strange men who ring out of nowhere. Good—"

"*Non, non, pardonnez moi. Écute moi, por fa*vor. I see how it seems, but I am in need of the help of a private dick."

I didn't much like his description of my calling.

5

Too 1950s Hollywood. I took a breath to calm down and gather my thoughts. "Very well, I'll listen, but I'm going to need a good deal more information before I agree to meet with you. Shall we start with your name?"

"I am Francois Ketchak. I am the owner of Ketchak's Funfair which is in Haxford for the Wool Fair. *Tu comprends*?"

"I understand. And what is it I can do for you, Monsieur Ketchak?"

"My life. It is being threatened."

That did not make sense. This was Haxford not Sicily...or Chicago... or even Corsica. Haxford did not do death threats unless you counted those made by me on Dennis, but they were usually the result of some misdemeanour on his part, like walking into the house without taking off his working boots first.

"Go to the police."

"I do not wish to waste the time of your British *Polizei*, madame, for what may be no more than a lazy threat. I ask again, would it be possible for you to meet me?"

"Not so fast, monsieur. Please listen to me. I know what I'm talking about. I was a police officer for many years." I didn't think it necessary to tell him that I left the police service almost thirty years ago. The law hadn't changed that much. "Death threats are a matter for them, not a private investigator."

"But I don't know that it is serious, Madame, and I do not want to risk them turning on me. I need your help and to explain, I need to speak to you in person."

I resigned myself to the fact that he was not going to go away. "All right, but there are two things you should understand. I charge twenty pounds for an initial consultation, non-refundable, and it's my decision whether or not I take your case. Are you all right with that?"

"*Si.*"

"In that case, I can meet you as long as it's in Haxford, and in a public place, yes."

"I am at the Haxford Arms on *la Rue de Huddersfield. Oui?* You know it?"

I checked the clock and read half past nine. "I'll see you in the lounge bar at eleven o'clock. Is that okay?"

He agreed and I rang off.

M. Ketchak was not the only one who didn't want to waste his or even the police's time, hence my charge of twenty pounds for the initial consultation. As a rule, I charged nothing for the initial consultation, but there was something about this which was ringing bells at the back of my mind, bells that cried, 'forget it'.

On the other hand, comfortable though we were, Dennis and I were not so well off that I could afford to turn work away, and if there was anything to his claim, I still had enough friends and one son in the police to call for help.

With an hour and a half before our meeting, I decided I'd better make an effort on the dress front.

Cappy the Cat basked in the open doorway, occasionally dashing out to chase off a band of dangerous, life-threatening starlings, before returning to nuzzle up against me as if seeking approbation for his courage in the face of such adversity. Leaving him to his sentry duties, I went back to the bedroom and after giving the options some thought, took out my outfit for the meeting. I was wearing a pair of tight jeans, a loose fitting top bearing the legend, *I Luv Blondie*, and comfortable carpet slippers. I ditched those in favour of a sober, dark business suit and plain, opaque white blouse which would not (I hoped) show the line of my bra. Not that I didn't trust M. Ketchak, but he was French. I immediately castigated myself for the inherent racism in that thought. The French were no worse than your average, male Haxforder. On the other hand, our continental neighbours did have a reputation of being more romantic than your common or garden Yorkshireman. That would not take much doing. In Haxford, romance amounted to him asking, "Do you want salt and vinegar on your chips?"

Done dressing, I admired my trim-ish frame in the mirror, and I was satisfied. I looked the part of a professional woman selling her services to a client. Why did I always cringe at that thought? 'Professional woman' and 'selling her services' were open to too many interpretations.

Dennis, my husband, didn't understand this business of dressing appropriately. Not that there's anything unusual about him being unable to grasp such a concept. Unless he could take his spanners and tinker with it, he didn't understand anything. If I'd let him, he'd have turned up for our wedding in his boiler suit and steel-toe-capped boots, and I swear that if he ever fell seriously ill, those overalls would have to be surgically removed before they could treat him. He simply could not grasp the necessity of dressing to suit the occasion. The words 'dressing appropriately' needed to be taken in context. He did dress properly for his work. He's a mechanic; one of the best, and his job required overalls and safety boots. Trouble is, he couldn't see any other life than his work. If I told him the mayor had invited us to a formal reception, he'd go in his boiler suit and take his toolbox on the offchance that his worship's official limousine needed a quick tune up..

Dismissing thoughts of my husband's mechanical obsessions, I considered M. Ketchak instead.

I was not what could be called multilingual. I had a little Spanish, enough to be able to order food and drink in Benidorm, a smattering of French, sufficient to get me to the ladies lavatories at the Gare du Nord when we went to Paris on the Eurostar, and a teensy bit of German... I could count up to a hundred, but I only picked that up that when Simon was learning German at school.

Ketchak was good. His accent was convincing. At least as persuasive as Albert Finney or Peter Ustinov, but he made a couple of mistakes. I was certain that the French police were gendarmes, not Polizei. Or were they? Could it be that the ordinary bobbies were the Polizei and the gendarmes a special part of the police in France? A bit like the Anti-terrorist Branch in the UK? Even so, surely *la Rue de Huddersfield* would translate as Huddersfield Street, and the Haxford Arms was on

Huddersfield Road. Beyond that, *si* and *por favor* were Spanish, not French.

Something did not ring quite true, and I would need a lot of persuading before we reached any agreement. Not only that. I would need a recording of our conversation.

It took some time, but after rooting through the drawers of our display cabinet, I finally found my pocket recorder and one of the little cassette tapes to go with it. All I needed then were the batteries, and they took even more finding because I didn't have any. In a flash of inspiration, I pinched them from our TV and DVD player handsets and tested them in the recorder. Perfect, but I made a mental note to call in at Benny's Bargain Basement for new batteries on my way back from the Haxford Arms. I'd need those handsets working by the time Dennis got home from work. Robbing him of his remotes was like confiscating a child's toffees.

With the clock reading a little after half past ten, Cappy the Cat took exception to my ensuring he was in the house (that gang of feathered felons were still trying their luck in the garden) and the last I saw of him, he was sulking in his bed. Locking up, I climbed into my compact Renault and trundled out of the drive for the ten or fifteen minute drive to my rendezvous.

I had never heard of Ketchak's Funfair let alone Francois Ketchak, but that was no reason to doubt him. Haxford Wool Fair ran for a full week at the end of April, and every year it was a different funfair which settled into the lower corner of Barncroft's Meadow where the event was held. The upper part of the meadow was given over to more practical events, such as sheep shearing, sheepdog trials, and livestock shows, most of which involved sheep. Well, they would, wouldn't they? Back in the day, Haxford was part of the Heavy Woollen District, and the town only came into being thanks to sheep farming.

These days, we didn't process wool. It was baled up and shipped out somewhere (no point asking me where) before coming back ready for the squads of knitters spread across Great Britain, and a fair share of skeins, hanks and balls could be found on stalls at the Haxford Wool Fair. There were also stalls which sold finished products: jumpers, cardigans, matinee jackets for the little ones, and so on, and I recall one year a stall selling hand-knitted, woollen trousers and underwear. I don't think it did well. Dennis, for one, wouldn't entertain the idea.

"They sag when you climb out of the pool, do knitted swimming trunks."

When I asked how he knew, he wouldn't answer. I later learned that when he was at school, learning to swim, his mother knitted him a pair. Well, they were never a well-off family.

All this was going through my mind as I drove on autopilot down the steep hill into town, and then out again on Huddersfield Road until I turned into the large car park of the Haxford Arms.

Without checking up, I was convinced that the pub was the only place in town which offered bed and breakfast, and even then I guessed they would not be inundated with guests, not even on the eve of Haxford Wool Fair. The car park was all but empty, but amongst the few vehicles in there was a dark red, Toyota pickup truck, its sides emblazoned with the legend, *Ketchak's Funfair, fun for all the family*. Not particularly original, but I was impressed by the manner in which he managed to get all that along the side, especially when the headline, Ketchak's Funfair was written in a huge, flamboyant font, while the rest was so tiny that people like my husband would need reading glasses on.

I stepped into the lounge, and as I approached the bar, a tall-ish man got to his feet from a corner table, and approached. Maybe an inch or two shorter than Dennis's five feet eleven inches, he was dressed in a shabby, dark blue, pinstriped suit with a white shirt, the collar open, behind which was a red cravat. A ruddy complexion sported a bushy moustache, curled upwards at the edges, and under a head of dark hair, plastered in gel, brown eyes ran up and down me before fixing my gaze.

"Madame Capper?" As before, he pronounced it 'Cappeur'.

"Monsieur Ketchak?"

He snapped his heels to attention, took and kissed the back of my right hand. I'd rather he'd just shook hands, but I resisted the temptation to wipe my hand on my skirt.

"You would like a drink?"

"Just a glass of lemonade, please." I smiled an apology, "I'm driving."

"But of course." He gestured to the table where he had been sitting. "I will be *un moment*."

As I made my way to the table, I heard him ask for, '*Una limonada, et una cerveza, s'il vous plait*'.

The first thing on my list was to get to the truth about Francois Ketchak.

Chapter Two

We were on holiday in Benidorm a few years back and we called at a café for breakfast. Unfortunately the young woman serving us didn't speak English. A rarity in Benidorm, but there you are. Dennis took it upon himself to order in pidgin Spanish delivered with a thick, Yorkshire accent. I remember the conversation quite well.

"*Tossed-a-does et manter-keeler, et tea con lechery, pour favour.*"

The attendant frowned. "*Que?*"

I felt it necessary to intervene before we fainted through lack of sustenance. "*Tostadas y mantequilla, y té con leche, por favor.*"

The girl beamed. "*Ah, señorita habla español.*"

"*Solamente un poco.*"

"*Buena. Tostadas y mantequilla, y té con leche. Por dos?*"

At this point Dennis, feeling a tad aggrieved at my intervention, butted in again. "No. It's all right, luv. We'll pour it ourselves."

I recalled that bizarre conversation as Ketchak joined me, settled into his seat with a glass of lager, and pushed a glass of lemonade across the table.

"So, Madame—"

I cut him off. "Not so fast. I need to lay down a

few ground rules, Monsieur Ketchak, the first of which is I will be recording this conversation." I dipped into my handbag and dropped the recorder on the table. "If you're unhappy with that, I'll leave now."

He shrugged. "It appears as if I do not have the *choix*."

"Good." I pressed the button to start the recording. "The second rule is that you must tell me the absolute truth."

"Of that, you have my assurance, Madame."

"Fine. In that case, why are you pretending to be French?"

He looked suitably offended. "You do me a great disservice, Madame. I come from a small village near Antibes in the *sud de la France*. From my family's home I could look upon the famous black and white lighthouse deep in the forest, or frolic in the surf *sur la plage de Contis*—"

"But you obviously never learned anything about geography," I interrupted. "The beach at Contis and its inland lighthouse figured in a French supernatural drama on BBC4 a couple of years ago. I watched it, and it's on the Atlantic coast of France, not the Mediterranean. Beyond that, Monsieur Ketchak, you've just ordered drinks in Spanish, and earlier you talked about the police in German, and mixed up 'Rue' and 'Route'. What next? Will you order lunch in Serbo-Croat?"

With a wary glance round the bar, he held up his hands, and when he spoke it was with a thick, Liverpool accent. "All right, all right, you've got me bang to rights, girl, but it's a front I have to put on for the punters. Yeah?"

Satisfied, I asked, "So your real name is…?"

"Frank Kilsby, and I'm from Bootle, Liverpool. The rest of me is kosher…ish. The company really is Ketchak's Funfair, we turned up the day before yesterday and we're standing the Haxford Wool Fair from tomorrow until the second of May, and my life has been threatened." With another furtive glance around the bar, he dipped into his pocket and came out with a sheet of A4 paper torn from a loose-leaf pad.

I held out my hand and when he tried to put the paper in it, I stopped him. "Make a gesture like twenty pounds dropping into my palm first. Consultation fee. Remember?"

He dipped into his inside pocket again, and this time came out with a tatty brown leather wallet, from which he withdrew a twenty and offered it. At once, the barman called across to us.

"Hey, you, don't be coming in here selling your… Oh. Sorry, Christine. I didn't realise it was you."

"I could take offence, Alec, but I'll let it pass this time. Do it again, and I'll make sure Dennis does a rubbish job the next time he services your car." The barman held up his hands in surrender, and I tucked the twenty in my bag.

Kilsby was impressed. "They obviously know you."

"Everyone knows me, Mr Kilsby, and they know not to mess with me." That sounded good. It was nonsense but I could see from his face that the message sank in. "You know my prices, you know the likelihood of success is low, you know the police should be called, but it doesn't alter the bill."

"I'm not short of a bob or two. Tell you what, if you're willing to take the job on, I'll make you a cheque out now. Let's say eleven days, which takes us from now until the end of the Wool Fair, two hundred notes a day. Call it two grand for round figures, and if you crack it early, I won't ask for a refund." His hand disappeared into the pocket again, and came out with a chequebook. Amazing. I didn't think people still used them. "How does that sound?"

It was tempting. Dennis's business made enough money to keep us comfortable, and I made a few pounds from my PI efforts and from sponsorship advertising for my vlog, but nothing like... I stopped myself. "It's too much. For all we know I might break this in two hours."

"All right then. We're just about set up and we open tomorrow, so how about I pay you for, let's say, two days at two hundred a day, and we can take it from there."

I agreed. It was probably still too much, but I wasn't going to sit here all day haggling.

He wrote out the cheque and handed it over. I made sure everything was ticketyboo and tucked it in my bag with the twenty.

"You know, it occurs to me that I've just taken your money and I haven't yet agreed to take the case. As a matter of interest, how did you get to know about me?"

"One of the foodies standing the fair. We set up the attractions, but there are some stalls which are nothing to do with us, and the fast food stands are among them. This was some woman called Sandra. Had two blokes in overalls helping her set up her pitch."

I was puzzled. I did not know anyone called Sandra. "No surname?"

"She must have, but I didn't catch it. Calls her van Sandra's Snacky."

Of course I knew a Sandra: Sandra Limpkin who ran Sandra's Snacky in the mill where Dennis and his business partners had their premises. The thought of Haxford Mill, Sandra and Dennis produced a mental impression of the two men in overalls Kilsby mentioned, and one of them had to be my old man. But if Sandra was standing Haxford Wool Fair, who was running the café in the mill?

I didn't have time to think about it as Kilsby asked, "You say you're an ex-copper."

"I am."

"Still got contacts on the force?"

"Some, but they won't help."

"I'm thinking in terms of the scuffers poking their nose in when you identify this scroat. I'd rather kick seven bells out of him personally."

As slang for the police, 'scuffers' was a term I hadn't heard in years, and I had an idea it was limited to Merseyside. In an effort to stamp out these mental distractions, I held my hand out for the sheet of paper and he laid it on the table, from where I picked it up and read it.

YOUR SCUM. YOU WONT SEE THE WALPURGIS AT THE WUL FARE.

It looked like it had been written in red, felt pen.

The handwriting was spidery and (deliberately?) shaky.

One thing leapt out at me. "It's odd that they spelled 'you're', 'wont', 'wool' and 'fair' wrong, yet got Walpurgis right."

Kilsby frowned. "Have they? I wouldn't know. I don't know anyone called Walpurgis."

"It's not a person—"

"In that case, I've never been to Walpurgis."

"It's not a place, either," I assured him. "It's a religious festival, and I'm sure it's been taken over by pagans, an excuse for orgies."

"Really? Well, that lets me out. I don't do orgies, and I'm not from Paga, and I don't think I've ever been there, wherever it is. I'm a Scouser."

Not for the first time, I questioned his general intelligence. Putting that to one side, I asked, "What makes you think this is serious and not someone trying to wind you up?"

"Well, I said didn't I, that I've never heard of Wal… whatever it's called, but after what you've just told me about religions and this Paga place, there must be some of the crew who have. Forgetting that, I run a tight ship. People do as they're told or they scram. I'm not everybody's best friend, and most people work the fair on a cash in hand basis. It could be that someone I've booted out is determined to get his own back. All I need you to do is poke around, ask questions, compare handwriting and stuff. The kind of thing you gumshoes do. Then point me in the right direction, and I'll deal with it. Yeah?"

On the phone I had been a private dick and now I

was a gumshoe. Whatever next? A shamus? He made me feel as if I should go out and buy a trench coat and fedora. It didn't need to be expensive. I already had a trench coat, but it was one of the modern ones, not a hangover from a Bogart movie, and as for the fedora... I suppose the effect wouldn't be the same with one of Dennis's flat caps.

"You're convinced it's one of the people who work or has worked on the fair?"

He shrugged and gulped down some lager. "Who else could it be? We're on the move all the time, Mrs C—"

"Please call me Christine."

"Christine. It's rare that we're in any one place for more than a fortnight, so I never get to know the locals. I mean, we've just left Oswestry, and when we're through with the Wool Fair, we're on our way to Carlisle. It's the job, see. That's what it is. On the move all the time. The only time we're static is during January and February, but we were set up in Liverpool before Christmas, and we only went back on the road at the beginning of March." He leaned forward. "Listen, luv, you're smart. I mean, how long did it take for you to realise I'm not French?"

"Not long." I didn't think there was much point in telling him it was because he had less intelligence than Cappy the Cat. No point in antagonising the customer at such an early stage, especially when I had a cheque for £400 in my purse. Not that I'm mercenary or anything, but as Dennis was often keen to stress, you should, "Never look a gift horse in the mouth and whatever you do, don't kick its teeth in."

"There you are then. You notice things."

Kilsby's words brought me back to the here and now. Matters were moving at a pace, but it was time to rein him in a little. "I feel I must point out, Mr Kilsby—"

"I prefer Frank."

"All right, Frank. I must point out that I don't get into confrontations."

"No problem, girl. I'll do the confrontationing. All you have to do is point the finger."

"If I can." Why was I so cautious with him? I should be telling him that I was certain of pointing the finger. Before he could pick me up on that, I asked, "When do you move into Barncroft's Meadow?"

"Barncroft's Mead…? Oh. You mean the field where we're standing? I just said, we're already there. We shipped in two days ago, and we open for business tomorrow. That's how long it takes to set up and make sure everything's working as it should be."

"Okay. So if I go down there now, I can start talking to people, can I?"

Doubt crossed his face. "Well, I'd rather they didn't know I was hiring you."

Once again, questions were raised on his intelligence. "It'll be difficult finding the culprit if I'm not allowed to talk to them, Frank."

"No, I don't mean you can't, but you can do it incognisant, can't you? You know? Undercover. I mean, that's what you pro-Sherlocks are all about, innit?"

So I was a Sherlock now. I wondered if he'd never heard the word shamus. "Well, I suppose I could pose as a reporter. I mean, my vlog is well-known in Haxford."

"So Sandra wossname said. What's a vlog? Some kind of motor scooter or something?"

He was obviously not au fait with the world of the internet and probably less au fait with *au fait*. "It's a video blog. I put out a fifteen minute video every week, and this week, with the start of Haxford Wool Fair, it gives me the perfect excuse to poke around."

"There you go then. A verloggist you are." He drained off his beer. "If you wanna follow my truck, we can get on down there."

I agreed, drank my lemonade and paid a visit to the ladies before climbing into my car and following him out of the car park and back towards town.

As always, the roads were busy, and there was a series of traffic lights between the Haxford Arms and the town centre bypass. We had to stop twice waiting for them to change in our favour. As he approached the third set on the bypass right outside the police station, they changed at the last possible moment. His brake lights lit up, but he didn't stop. He careened on, yanked his wheel to the right to avoid the stationary car ahead of him, and with smoke coming from his rear wheels, the result of pulling on his parking brake, he ran into the bollard at the lights.

Chapter Three

With traffic stopping on the opposite carriageway to see what was going on and a queue building up in both lanes behind us, I pulled in behind Kilsby, tucking my car tight to the right hand lane, put my hazard flashers on, climbed out, rushed to him and yanked open his door.

He was lolling forward, forehead resting on the steering wheel, shaking, his fingers white, clamped around the wheel. "Rotten brakes failed, didn't they? I thought they were soft when I pulled off the pub car park."

This was a job for Dennis. I dug out my smartphone, and I was about to call him, when bodies emerged from the police station and hurried across the road. They were led by Sergeant Vic Hillman, a man who never had much time for me when I was on the force. That was after I learned of a car named a Hillman Minx, and I nicknamed him appropriately.

"Get your car shifted, Capper."

"I'm with—"

Hillman didn't give me time to explain. He turned on the three constables accompanying him. "You two, traffic control, you, get back in the station and bring out the breathalyser." He turned again, this time on Kilsby. "I don't know how much you had to drink, pal, but—"

I cut him off for once. "Shut your mouth and open your ears for once, Vic. I've been with him for the last half-hour, and he's had one small beer. He's not drunk. His brakes failed."

"And how many times did you hear that when you were one of us?"

"Are you calling me a liar?"

"If the cap fits... especially while you're out with some bloke while Dennis's back is turned."

I was on the verge of losing my temper. It didn't happen often, but people like Vic Hillman were skilled at testing my reserve, and that last remark was calculated to push me to the limit. While the two constables set about getting the traffic moving on both sides of the carriageway, I walked away, holding my breath, mentally counting to ten. I stopped at the rear of Kilsby's truck, and stared down at the road. My car was a yard behind him, but in that small gap, I could see a trail of what looked like fresh oil but which I guessed was brake fluid.

A nasty little smile creased my lips. "Hey, Minx, take a look at this."

Calling him by the soubriquet he detested didn't do me any favours. His face suffused with colour and he almost ran to me. "If you call me Minx again..."

"And if you call me Capper again, you'll know about it. It's Christine, Chrissy or Mrs Capper to you." I pointed down at the carriageway. "Brake fluid? Or do you imagine he wet himself while he was driving and it dripped through the floor?" I didn't wait for an answer. "I think his brake pipes have been cut." I took out my smartphone again. "You do what you want with him, but I tell you now, he's not drunk. I'll ring Dennis, get him to tow the pickup away."

"No way. That needs investigating by one of our—"

I interrupted again. "Dennis is authorised to carry out police inspections. Remember?"

Dennis had been okayed by the police for some time. His was the only business in Haxford making use of a tow truck which could handle anything up to medium sized vans. Anything bigger and they had to send for heavy gear from Huddersfield. Aside from that, Dennis was well-known as a top-flight mechanic. He could tell you what was wrong with a car just by listening to it. It's a pity he couldn't employ the same skills with me – listening and diagnostic – but as I'm so fond of saying, you can't have everything, can you?

At this point, Hillman backed off. "All right. Get him out. But I'm still gonna breathalyse him."

I scored that round to me on points, and rang Dennis.

"I'm busy. What do you want, Chrissy?"

"I need you and your wrecker on the bypass outside the police station. Minor bump. Police think he's drunk. I know he's not, but you'll need to check his car over."

I could hear a lot of noise in the background, and it sounded like the rattling engine of Dennis's wrecker, compounded by other noises, almost as if he were working on a building site, and that was impossible. There were no building sites anywhere near his workshop.

"It'll take a while. I told you, I'm busy."

"Busy doing what?"

"I've just dropped Sandra's snack van at Barncroft's Meadow. She's standing the Wool Fair."

Kilsby had mentioned her but what did it have to do with my husband? Before I asked, I knew I had got it right when Kilsby mentioned two men in overalls. "Sandra Limpkin?"

"Do you know any other Sandras? She's hired a van for the fair, and she asked me to tow it there. She put some geek onto you while we were setting her up, me and Grimy."

Totally innocent then. It always was with Dennis. "I'm with that geek now." Or was it totally innocent. "I suppose you're setting Sandra up as a freebie?"

"Payment in kind," he confessed with a smile in his voice. "And before your mind runs off in the wrong direction, I'm charging her a tenner plus free breakfasts for the week, for me, Geronimo, and Grimy."

Geronimo and Grimy were Dennis's business partners, Tony Wharrier and Lester Grimes.

"All right. How long, Dennis? Only the road's busy and Minx is getting in a state."

"As it happens, I'm in the wrecker. I used it to tow Sandra's van to the fairground. I'll have to drop Grimy back at the mill, so let's say, twenty minutes, half an hour."

"I'll wait here for you." I cut the call and reported to Hillman who was in an even worse mood after the breathalyser proved negative.

"Are you gonna wait here for Dennis?" He wanted to know.

"Yes. In any case, assuming you're not gonna detain Kilsby for having the audacity to crash outside the police station, I'll have to take him down to Barncroft's Meadow." I saw the scowl appear again. "He's a client."

"Oh, yes. Flogging it now, are you?"

That was an insult too far. Even when I was younger, I was never that kind of girl. A couple of WKDs with a man I liked, maybe, but I never... "I don't care how big you are, Vic Hillman, one more crack like that and I'll put you on sick leave."

Leaving the police to handle traffic, I climbed into the passenger seat alongside Kilsby.

He gave me a weak half smile. "Now do you believe me?"

"Your story is looking more likely, Frank, but we're waiting for my husband. He'll take your truck back to his place and have a look at it. He's authorised by the police to assess these things, and you'll get his report at the same time as the police. I don't know much about vehicle systems, but it looks like your brake lines have been cut. Trust me, Dennis is the best. He'll get to the bottom of it."

"Is he expensive?"

"The cheapest in Haxford." I didn't see the point in telling him that Dennis was the *only*, properly qualified auto-engineer in town. Haxford Fixers, the name of his business, employed only three people –

Dennis, Tony, and Lester – but small as it might be, it was the only company geared up for any and every automobile eventuality. After them, customers would be left with a handful of one-man bands working out of little sheds, or mechanics carrying out foreigners in their spare time, and Haxford Fixers' nearest serious competitors were in Huddersfield.

Kilsby looked out at the police and gave a half-hearted, cynical chuckle. "Good job I hadn't had more to drink, isn't it?"

"How long were you at the Haxford Arms before I got there?"

"An hour. I wasn't drinking. I had a good breakfast and a cuppa before you turned up." He laughed again. "I'm not stupid. I know how keen the filth are when it comes to booze, and I've fired one or two hands for being full of ale when they're manning the rides."

That sparked my interest. "Can you think of anyone who might have followed you to Haxford?"

He shook his head. "If they have, I haven't seen them."

With the traffic building up during the noon rush, it was all hands to the police pumps to sort the traffic out, and we were receiving glares of sheer hatred many drivers when they managed to squeeze past. I got sick of returning apologetic stares, so looked away to concentrate on Kilsby.

"Frank, how were your brakes on the way to the pub?"

"Good. Nothing wrong with them as far as I could tell." He waved at the gridlocked road. "I mean, this is a busy little place. Traffic stopping and starting every two hundred yards, but I didn't notice any problem with the anchors."

"If I'm right then, and Dennis will tell us, it means someone must have cut the pipes after you got there, while you were having breakfast or while we were talking."

"With the best will in the world, missus, I didn't need to pay you four hundred notes to work that out. All you have to do is finger him and leave him to me."

I tutted. "He – or she – has broken the law. It's a serious offence. When Dennis reports to the police, they won't let it go that easily."

"Don't worry about it, girl. I'll leave enough for the cops to deal with... once he gets out of hospital."

This was worse than talking to Dennis. At least he just didn't listen.

And talking of my husband, he turned up twenty minutes later, pointing in the wrong direction, and held up traffic across all four lanes while he shunted his wrecker round and reversed up to Kilsby's pickup. Then, because the pickup was jammed into the bollard near the traffic lights, he had to get me to move my car back several yards, which involved a number of police officers forcing the traffic to funnel into the one free lane sooner than they would have liked. From there, he had to get Kilsby and Hillman to help him push the pickup back off the bollard so he had room to lower what he called an A-frame to the ground, and then he needed a push to get the pickup's front wheels onto said A-frame.

Once having secured it in place, he climbed into his cab and hoisted the pickup's front up, ready for towing away.

Leaving his engine running, he joined us again. "Right, Minx, who am I billing for this?"

Hillman's face turned near purple. "I've warned your missus once. Don't call me Minx."

"Well your mam should have married a different bloke, shouldn't she?"

That constituted another brace of Dennis's problems. Common sense and diplomacy. He didn't employ the former and he never learned the latter.

"And leave my old queen out of this."

"Just tell me who I'm billing."

Hillman pointed at Kilsby. "Him. It's his car. But we want a report."

Dennis nodded. "So that's the assessment and repair to you, pal," he said to Kilsby, "and a copy of the report and a twenty quid bill to you, Min… Sarge."

"Twenty quid?" If Hillman got any more shocks, I swear he would have a stroke.

Dennis smiled mock-sweetly. "Admin charges."

All credit to my husband. He was never behind the door when it came to making a pound or two. He knew very well that the police would pay without question, and I'd seen his 'reports' before. If I had this right, this one would read something like, 'The brake pipes were cut'. It would be handwritten and signed but he wouldn't even post it. Spend money on stamps? Not likely. He'd scan it and email it to them.

The police hands were tied. They would need

that assessment. Considering the chaos this minor accident had caused, someone would have to take the blame. If the brake lines really were cut, there'd be a criminal investigation, but if it was down to shoddy maintenance, then it was Kilsby's responsibility and he would be prosecuted.

Whistling cheerfully to himself, Dennis climbed into his wrecker and drove away. I'm sure I heard a cheer go up from the queuing motorists. Hillman spent a few minutes taking a statement from Kilsby, and we climbed into my car and joined the easing throng for the journey to Barncroft's Meadow.

"There was one question I never asked," I said as I settled into the steady moving line of traffic. "You suspect a member of your crew."

"Even more so now. I mean, who else would know where to find my truck at this hour?"

"How many people knew you'd be at the Haxford Arms?"

"Well, er, none. I just said I had to go out."

"Then, in theory, it could have been anyone passing. To get back to what I was saying, you suspect one of your crew. So who amongst them would threaten to kill you?"

"Er... A good few of them, I suppose. I'm a hard taskmaster, Christine. I like things right, and if it ain't right, I shout and bully them into getting it right."

"And this is your regular crew, is it?"

"Mostly. One or two locals, sure. We put out a call for them the other week, through the employment services – not keen because our jobs are mainly cash in hand – and your local rag. The

Recorder, is it? Grafters and gophers, mainly. Sweeping up and clearing the litter bins."

At the bottom of the bypass, where it turned east to loop round the town, I followed the right hand fork for Derbyshire Road. From here it would drop down into the valley where it met again with the sluggish stream we called the River Hax, and then climb the hills to the moors north of Glossop.

His last answer intrigued me. "Sweeping up and litter picking? Don't the council do that?"

He laughed. "They would have done, but you should have seen how much they wanted. Crikey, they charged us the earth for standing in this field."

"That's sounds about right for Haxford Borough Council. So, do you own the fair outright?"

"The bigger attractions, yeah. Most of the sidestalls are owned by the operators, but they've been with me for yonks. We're just one, big, happy family."

"Judging by what happened to your brakes, I'd say someone isn't so happy."

Chapter Four

At the bottom of a long dip in the road stood the entrance to Barncroft's Meadow. There was nothing formal or signposted about it, no five-bar gate or anything. It was just a large gap in the trees and bushes lining the right hand side of the road.

On the way down, looking above the treeline, I could see bits and pieces of the fair jutting up into the clear sky. They were slotting together the little spire on top of the helter-skelter, and further over I could see men – I assume they were men – putting the finishing touches to the two towers for what's known as the slingshot or reverse bungee. You were strapped into a little cage and they shot you into the air. You came zooming back down on bungee ropes which bounced up and down until you were ready to throw up, at which point they pulled you down to earth. In Blackpool it was called the Skyscreamer and speaking for myself, I think I'd vomit as I climbed into the cage. Not that I ever would. I like the occasional thrill, but I prefer them to be on terra firma, not flying all over Barncroft's Meadow on rubber ropes. And talking of thrills on terra firma, Barncroft's Meadow did have that kind of reputation when the Wool Fair was not in town... not that I speak from experience, naturally.

As I turned in, the open area immediately before us was in the final stages of transformation into a parking area. This included the siting of rows of portaloos – all coin operated – and large signs indicating that parking would be charged at £5 per day. Good old Haxford Borough Council. Not content with charging Ketchak's Funfair a small fortune for using the field, they would rip off the visitors for the privilege of parking on a patch of grass, and then charge them again for using the smallest room, and in the case of these portable potties, I do mean smallest.

Frank had sunk into a contemplative or perhaps worried silence after we passed through the town, and even now, he didn't speak, just pointed towards a gap in the trees ahead of us. It was a rough track where courting couples would meander through and into the meadow proper. Yes, and in amongst those trees, they'd indulge in the occasional spot of…well, I don't need to draw a diagram, do I?

Beyond the small copse, the meadow opened out into a vast, flattish expanse of grass. Way over to the right, larges areas were roped off and giant marquees were already in place. That's where the sheepdog trials, shearing, and livestock shows would be held. Curiously enough, or maybe not so curious for a town where sheep farming and wool had always been king, those events were quite popular with the middle-aged and older Haxforders.

Immediately in front of us, however, was the main attraction of Haxford Wool Fair; the funfair, now at an advanced stage of testing… all but for the slingshot where the steeplejacks looked as if they were taking down one of the ropes. The waltzer and dodgems were readily recognisable, further out was the screamer (as opposed to skyscreamer) a ride comprising individual cars on pivots, which were almost on their side when the ride circled at its maximum speed. There was also the cyclone, where the carriages went round and up and down, and spun in alternate directions, three to an arm. There were other adult rides and I noticed a ghost train, which was unusual for a travelling fair.

"Complicated set up," Kilsby admitted. "My daughter mans it but I have to supervise when we're setting up because I'm the only one who knows how it all goes together. Takes a full day to build it and get all the electrics and animatronics working proper. Worth it, mind. It gets a lot of custom."

Aside from those, there were several children's rides; a couple of roundabouts, the aforementioned helter-skelter, and the teacups roundabout, which I always felt was inspired by the un-birthday party in Alice in Wonderland, and which I knew my granddaughter, Bethany, would love.

I spotted Sandra Limpkin fussing about in her van, sited between the hook-a-duck stall and something called a 'penalty shootout' where punters had to knock over a hinged, wooden footballer by kicking the ball at him. Fortunately the shootout stall had surrounding nets or Sandra might have been in for a torrid time. Burgers, buns, and hot drinks didn't mix well with flying footballs.

There were other food stalls: a space earmarked for a hot dog stand, another for chips, candy floss and toffee apples, popcorn, soft drinks, pick and mix sweets and although I couldn't see any, I knew there would be at least two ice cream vans.

And there were the usual sidestalls; darts, hoopla, a .22 shooting gallery, water gun, where you had to direct a high-pressure jet of water into a clown's open mouth to inflate and (hopefully) burst a balloon, and almost inevitably, there was a fortune teller's tent, the sign outside advising prospects that Romany Márta Mitrea would 'reveal all'. It was a poor choice of words, conjuring images of a seedy burlesque show, but I was sure it meant palm reading, crystal ball, your future in the tarot.

"Is she really a gypsy?" I asked as Kilsby guided me slowly through the various rides towards the accommodation caravans.

"Only inasmuch as we're never in one place for longer than a fortnight. Her real name's Martha Mitchell, and she comes from Runcorn, not Rumania."

As I watched this activity, people working here and there, preparing for the feast to come, I felt a distant inkling of the excitement I had known first as a child and later as a fly teenager pretending to be a tearaway and out for an evening of fun. I remembered the times when Dennis and I brought our two children, Simon and Ingrid, to the fair, their excitement echoing mine of younger years. Dennis could take or leave it. He liked to look at the engines driving the various rides, but that's Dennis. When we were on holiday, while other people took photographs of the hotels, the beach, the general area, and fellow holidaymakers, Dennis took pictures of cars, buses and lorries.

Kilsby guided me past the waltzer and dodgems and down towards the river's edge where the crew's accommodation vans were located. They were roped off with signs hanging here and there warning visitors that there was no admittance. A collection of maybe two dozen caravans, and there was nothing flash or fancy about them. They were similar to those on any holiday park in the country, except that these were mobile, not static. There was another difference. No self-respecting holiday park would offer accommodation in clapped out rubbish like this. Most of them needed attention to the side panels and door, and even a coat of paint would do wonders for them.

"Haven't time," Kilsby said when I commented. "Besides, I don't own the vans… Well, not all of them. Just two." He aimed a finger at the two brighter, smarter vans in the centre of the semicircle. "Me and the missus in one, the other one is my daughter, her lad, and whichever boyfriend she's with at any one time."

He pointed to the second van where a young man of about fifteen was trying to empty kitchen waste from a bin into in a black bag, and not making a good job of it. Potato peelings, cabbage leaves and such, empty cans and bottles poured out of the bin and mostly across the immediate ground. "Gina's not in. Her bike's missing. But that's Nick, my grandson. Nick is short for Nicholas, and short is the right word for him. Hasn't enough brain cells to strike a spark."

I parked the car at the ropes and we climbed out. As we approached his van, a sleeping German

Shepherd, anchored to the van by a strong chain, came to its senses and barked at me.

"Get down, barmpot," Kilsby snapped at it, and the dog flopped to the ground, ears pricked, eyes following both of us. It was suspicious of me, but I swear it resented him.

The door was open. Kilsby led the way in and I followed, and as he stepped in, he called out, "It's only me, Rache. Get the kettle on. We've got a visitor."

A woman appeared from our right, presumably the bedroom area.

Kilsby beamed on her. "Rache, this is Christine Capper, a local reporter sort. Christine, this is my wife, Rachel."

We shook hands but contrary to Kilsby's breezy friendliness, she was sour-faced and her flaccid grip indicated she would be happier to throw me out than welcome me in.

I guessed her to be about forty, a good fifteen years younger than Kilsby, whose age I'd learned was fifty-five. He had to give his date of birth in his police statement (yes I was listening in when he spoke to Hillman). Flat-chested with a spreading behind and what I imagined were chunky legs hidden in a pair of loose-fitting jogging pants, she had a shock of untidy, red hair, urgently in need of a brush, comb, and a squirt of Harmony. Green eyes flashed fire at me, and if her lips had been turned down any further they'd have passed for an impression of her husband's moustache only lower down her face.

"Reporter?" she asked. The thick, scouse voice

was just as sour as the rest of her.

"Actually, I'm a well-known vlogger and blogger, and I'm covering the Wool Fair this week. My readers and viewers will be fascinated by the background to the funfair."

"Will they?"

I could see this woman would take some convincing.

She concentrated on her erstwhile. "Well here's some background for you, Frank. Ossie says one of the bungee ropes is frayed on the slingshot. Either get a new one or it doesn't play, and he says that by rights, you should do both ropes just to be sure."

"Aw for the love of..." I anticipated a stream of Anglo-Saxon but in deference to me (I think) he cut it off. Instead, he fumed in silence for a moment then took out his phone. He jabbed the necessary button and put it to his ear. "Ossie? I'm in my van. Get over here."

Rachel wasn't finished yet and as Kilsby dropped the phone back in his pocket, she asked, "Where's your truck?"

"Fender bender," he said. "Christine helped me out. Gave me a lift back here."

Rachel stared at him in a manner which I'm sure accused him of something he hadn't done (and which, I have to say, he'd never have got the chance to do with me) and I stood by in half embarrassed silence, waiting for her to explode. It didn't happen. A minute later, the door opened again and a Greek god stepped in.

Would I climb over Dennis to get to him? In a flash.

And this was so unusual for me. I don't look at other men. A woman in a stable marriage for as long as ours should entertain no fantasies starring other men, and I have to say, Dennis never daydreamed of other women. Their cars, yes, but not them. This individual was an exception proving the rule.

About six feet six, wearing jeans and a tight, black vest, he was lean, mean, and all meat, strapping muscles flexing, ready to scoop me off the floor and carry me away... actually, I was getting carried away without his help. He was closer to Rachel's age than Kilsby's, a good looking man, designer stubble on his chisel chin, soft and persuasive blue eyes with a hint of humour in them. He scanned the room, scanned me and gave me an alluring sign of welcome before Kilsby introduced us.

"This is Christine Capper. She's a blocker and she's doing a piece on the fair. Christine, this is Ossie Travis."

We shook hands and Ossie's massive paw buried my hand past my wrist.

"Blocker?" he asked. "You play American football?"

"He means blogger."

Kilsby stepped in before we could properly chat. "Never mind what I mean. What's this about the bungee ropes?"

If Ossie was at all intimidated, he did a good job of hiding it. "I've been telling you about it for months. I warned you through the winter, but you didn't wanna listen. You can't use it, Frank. If you do and it snaps, you'll end up doing time for criminal negligence, and I ain't carrying the can for you."

Sweat broke on Kilsby's brow. "Where am I gonna get another bungee rope?"

"The nearest supplier I know of is in Bolton," Ossie assured him. "And to be safe, you shouldn't do the one rope. You should do them both."

Kilsby didn't need telling that Rachel had already apprised him of Ossie's opinion, but I seemed to recall Dennis saying something similar about vehicle suspension systems. He always insisted that when one side went, both should be replaced. And there was I thinking it was just Dennis's way of milking the customer for more money, but the hunk here was saying the same about his bungee ropes.

Kilsby looked on the verge of losing it. "For god's sake..." He turned to me. "How far is it from here to Bolton?"

"Bolton?" I shrugged. "Forty, fifty miles. Maybe more."

"Right. I'll have to go over there and get one. Ossie, my truck's off the road so you'll have to drive me. Sorry, Christine, but this is an emergency and I'll have to leave you with Rachel."

"No problem. I need to speak to a few people anyway."

He disappeared into one of the other rooms while Rachel moved to the worktop to make some tea. A few minutes later, he was back having dumped his suit and put on jeans and a sweatshirt.

"I'm on me way, Rache. I'll be three hours.

Maybe longer."

"Don't rush on my account." Kilsby disappeared and as she made tea, Rachel asked, "So, you gave him a lift?"

"It was the least I could do."

She looked me up and down. "You're sure that's all you gave him?"

If this woman thought she had the exclusive on nasty, she had another think coming. "If he'd tried for anything else, I'd have cut his gropey hands off." I took a deep breath. "I can see that you don't like me, Rachel, but I don't play games like you're suggesting and I don't understand why you'd think that."

She shrugged, and she carried two cups to a small table. "I don't know you, but I know Frank. If it wears a skirt, it's fair game." The mean eye fell on me again. "You wouldn't be the first."

"Believe me, I wouldn't be last either, I wouldn't even be on the list."

I sipped the weak tea and looked around.

Standard caravan furnishings, everything compacted for space saving. Cushions strewn here and there. Odd items of clothing left lying around, the wall-side settees and chair coverings dirty, a selection of unwashed pots at the sink side, I felt the urge to whip home, pick up my cleaning gear and the Dyson and set about it.

"These are just your summer quarters are they?"

"All year round," she replied. "Even in winter we live in this dump." The sneer came back. To her voice. "You don't know what that's like, do you? I suppose yours is a two-up, two down, des res, is it?"

"A bungalow, actually." Why did I suddenly feel guilty about my home? Dennis and I worked hard for it, but I suspect not as hard as this woman worked.

"So how come you were there when he bumped his truck?"

"I met him in a pub by arrangement, and as we came out—"

"Ah. So you're the private eye he was meeting."

So much for incognito, or incognisant, as Kilsby put it.

"You knew?"

"Look around you, missus." She waved a flaccid hand at the caravan. "You can't have secrets in a place like this. And it's about this crackpot message he got, isn't it? Someone threatening to rub him out?" Rachel did not wait for me to answer. "It's bull. It'll be someone he's wound up so they're getting their own back, putting the wind up him."

I thought of Dennis. I was tempted to tell her of my suspicions, but I decided there was no point. Not yet. Not until I knew, and Haxford Fixers was my next port of call. I remained noncommittal. "Maybe, maybe not. Either way, it's a threat and it's against the law. I know. I used to be a police officer."

She remained unimpressed. "Best thing you can do is forget it. Stick him with a bill for helping him with the bump and go back where you came from."

"He's already paid me, Rachel, and I don't back away from things like this."

"Suit yourself."

In an effort to appease her, I explained, "I really

am a blogger and vlogger, though, and the fair does interest me. What exactly do you do?"

She sniffed. "I man the ticket booth." When I passed on my puzzlement in the shape of a frown, she went on. "People don't hand over money to go on the rides. They buy tickets at a booth when they come in. One-twenty-five a ticket or they can buy a book of twenty-five for twenty nicker, or eighty for sixty quid. The kids' rides cost two tickets per child or adult. The bigger rides anything up to five tickets. At the end of the fair, the stallholders or ride owners hand over their tickets and we settle up the cash equivalent... minus their share of the site rent. We get most of the arguments from the sidestall owners. At two tickets a time, they don't take a fortune, and the rents can be a bit steep."

"Does that include the food stalls?" I only asked because I couldn't see Sandra Limpkin faffing about with tickets. She played for hard cash.

Rachel shook her head. "They're mostly local yokels and they take cash. Same goes for Martha, the so-called fortune teller. A law unto herself, that one. She charges the punters a tenner and we bill her for the rent." She gave a disdainful little grunt. "Fortune teller? She couldn't forecast the winner in a one-horse race." Rachel finished her tea. "I'll tell you again, if you're looking for someone ready to bump Frank off, you'll have a cast of thousands... including me and Gina."

"Gina?"

"His daughter? Get that? *His* daughter, not mine. She came along about three months after he married his first wife."

"And that first wife is no longer around?"

"Dumped him after less than two years. Left him high and dry with the brat. He had a line of women after that until I turned up ten years ago, and I was the only one daft enough to marry him."

Chapter Five

After leaving Rachel, I walked over for a quick word and a cup of decent tea with Sandra Limpkin, but she was too busy setting up to spare me much time, so with the clock reading a few minutes to two, I left the meadow and drove back towards town, but veered off for Haxford Mill.

The Barncroft family, who owned most of Haxford at one time, always insisted that the town only came into being because of the mill, and when the last of the family died out, their land and property were bequeathed to the local council on condition that they made no alterations to the exterior of any building, amongst which were the cottage hospital, formerly the Barncroft manor house, the public library, where I had been dragged into the search for the Graveyard Poisoner, and the mill, on the back of which, the Barncrofts made their fortune. Haxford Borough Council had no problem with the restrictions imposed by the last of the Barncrofts for the simple reason that they never had enough money to alter the outside of any building. There was plenty of spare cash for the odd council junket to Limoges, Haxford's twin town, but none for local works.

It always remained a mystery to me how we

became twinned with Limoges, which was best known for its porcelain. How did you square porcelain and wool? The council's argument went something like, 'there are textile outlets in Limoges'. Fine. I'm sure there were some in Sheffield, too, but it was better known for steel.

Be that as it may, Haxford Fixers rented two large units on the ground floor of the mill, alongside the river. Not that you could see the river. There was a high wall between the mill and the Hax.

When I got there, the wrecker was parked alongside the firm's van, both sheltering Dennis's pride and joy, a 1979 Morris Marina which he'd rebuilt from scrap. When I walked into the workshop, Dennis was sat at his bench scribbling something on a sheet of paper, and Kilsby's pickup truck was over the pit, bonnet raised. At the rear of the workshop, Lester Grimes was working on an old tumble dryer, and from the other half of the premises, I could hear Tony Wharrier, the bodywork specialist, running a sander over something.

There was a time when Dennis and Tony worked for Addison's, the big auto specialists in Haxford. When they went bust, my husband and his pal set up Haxford Fixers and from the word go, they were inundated with work, not all of it on cars. Lester, an electrician, joined them later and if he specialised in general electrics, he was equally at home with the circuitry in cars and household appliances.

Although it was a three-way partnership, the three men didn't take equal pay from the job. Lester often complained that he made less than Dennis and

Tony, but they insisted it was because he was lazy. While they were there from 7:45 every morning, often working weekends, Lester would float in whenever he felt like it, and he tended to be extra late after a night on the beer and karaoke in the Engine House pub.

As a perfect demonstration of their different approaches, while Dennis was concentrated on whatever he was scribbling out, Lester was the one who noticed me first.

"Hey up, it's Chrissy Capper. Keeping an eye on the old man, are you, luv?" A mischievous glint came to his bloodshot eyes. "Or are you looking for a bit of spice? Huh? A rampant night with an old romeo? I'm free tonight."

"Well, I'm not. I have Dennis's dinner to cook."

At the sound of my voice, my husband looked up. "All right, lass? What are you doing here?"

"I came to see if you'd any news on Frank Kilsby's pickup."

"Just finished the report for plod."

"Yes. And?"

Dennis tutted. "It's supposed to be confidential, you know. I meanersay, I don't think—"

"That's right, Dennis, you don't ever think. You'll have to tell Kilsby. Are you going to make me wait until he gets back from Bolton?"

He frowned. "What's he doing in Bolton?"

Now I tutted. "Never mind what he's doing in Bolton. What about his vehicle?"

"Well, it's official. Someone cut the brake lines, and none to cleanly. Probably used a knife with a toothed edge."

"You mean serrated."

"All right then, a serrated knife with a toothed edge?"

I sighed again. With the best will in the world, there were times when… "Like a steak knife?"

"Spot on. And it'd have to be sharp, just like a steak knife."

I took the sheet from him and read his scrawl. The car number was there, a mention of the authorisation from Hillman. And underneath, he had written: *the brake pipes was cut close to both front wheels and successful use drained the reserver.*

I clucked. "Dennis, this is shocking. Bethany could do better and she hasn't started school yet."

"How do you mean?"

"It should be pipes *were* cut, and *successive* use and what does reserver mean? Reservoir?" I took his pen, struck out the offending words and put in the correct ones.

"So what am I?" he demanded. "A mechanic or an English teacher? As long as they understand."

"Just put it right and give me a copy. I'll take it to the police station."

"You don't have to," he said writing out the sheet for the second time. "I'll email it. I allus do."

"I still want a copy. I'll need to speak to Hillman or Mandy Hiscoe." Detective Sergeant Amanda Hiscoe was the senior CID officer in Haxford. For the time being anyway. She was something like five or six months pregnant, and no one knew who would step in when she took her maternity leave. Her baby was due in August, and according to my calculations she was entitled to maternity leave from mid-June, but I knew Mandy. Unmarried – who worried about such trivia these days – she was a workaholic and the chances were she would remain at her desk until a week or two before her due date.

Finished scribbling it out, Dennis scanned it and printed a copy for me. "I shouldn't think it's a CID job."

I folded the sheet in half and tucked it in my pocket. "You don't know the whole story, and I don't have time to tell you. I'll see you tonight and bring you up to speed." I nodded towards the body shop. "Give my regards to Tony. See you later, Lester," I called out as I left the building.

Lester called back to me, probably something ribald and unsuitable for mixed company, but I was outside by then and I didn't hear him.

Half past two and a grumbling tummy reminded me that I had had no lunch, so from Haxford Mill I drove into town, where I paid a quick call to the bank and deposited Frank Kilsby's cheque, and then made my way home, let Cappy the Cat out into the back garden, cut myself a tuna salad sandwich, and settled down in the conservatory where I watched our vicious sparrows and starlings tormenting Cappy the Cat from the upper reaches of the tall, back hedgerow.

It was only then that it occurred to me what a busy morning I had had; so busy that I hadn't found time to pick up batteries for our remote handsets. I rang Dennis and told him to collect some on his way home from work. I knew he'd forget but I could blame him when he couldn't get the classic car channel, or whatever channel it was where he watched repeats of *Top Gear*.

In the meantime, I had Frank Kilsby's problems to fill my time. Dennis's assessment meant that Kilsby was right. Someone meant him harm, and I had been well paid to find out who... if at all possible. Like it or not – and I didn't much like it – I had to go back to Barncroft's Meadow and begin that process.

The start of any such investigation was the worst. I had no suspects. Correction, I had a cast of a thousand suspects, starting with Rachel Kilsby. It didn't seem likely, but when I spoke to her, she didn't sound too keen on her old man, and looking beyond her, both she and her husband had admitted to a long, as yet unnamed list of people Kilsby had upset.

With my sandwich demolished, tea drunk, pots washed and put away, Cappy the Cat ordered back into the house (of the immediate tasks that proved the most difficult) I climbed back into the car and drove to the funfair for the second time, and it was just after quarter to four when I parked by the rope fencing of the accommodation trailers.

The dog barked at me again, and in my sternest voice, I ordered, "Shut up, Barmpot." The animal kept on barking and baring his teeth at me.

It never occurred to me that when Kilsby called the dog 'barmpot' he was cursing the beast rather than naming it. It only dawned on me when the dog ignored my instruction, and Nick, Gina's son, Frank's grandson, a specialist in making a mess with the kitchen waste, emerged from the adjacent van and told me, "He's not called barmpot. He's Kaiser."

I thanked him and looked at the dog again, but at that moment, Rachel came out and said, "Down, Kaiser," and the dog meekly obeyed. She then focussed on me. "What do you want this time?"

"Is your husband back?"

"Nope. Another hour at least."

"Oh. Can we talk?"

"What about?"

I only just stopped short of telling her that the correct phrase should be 'about what'. I didn't think she'd appreciate the lesson. "The threat to his life."

"I told you, it's twaddle."

"I don't think so, Rachel. I've just had the report on his minor bump this morning. The brake pipes on his car had been cut."

She did not appear too interested and I wondered what I had to do to move her to some level of concern. "You'd better come in."

Circling beyond the reach of the dog's chain, I followed her into the caravan where she switched the kettle on and prepared two beakers of tea. A few minutes later, when we were settled with a beaker each, I gave her the full rundown on my husband's assessment, and for all she cared, I might have been telling her that her nets needed washing. I mean, her nets did need washing, but given the state of the van, she obviously didn't care and the same applied to the sabotage of her husband's truck.

"You wouldn't know if anyone followed him to the pub this morning?"

"Nope. Coulda been anyone. Crew are on and off

the site all day. We're no different to anyone else, you know. We need to buy groceries and stuff. I was out myself this morning. I went to your local supermarket; CutCost is it? And Gina's been out half the day. She's checking out the clothes shops in town."

"Frank and his friend, Ossie, dropped her off?"

Rachel shook her head. "She has her own wheels. A Yammy 600."

It took a moment for me to work out that she was talking about a Yamaha 600 motorcycle, and I remembered Frank mentioning 'Gina's bike' missing. Determined to make a direct assault on her disinterest, I asked, "And would you or Gina have any reason to cut the brakes on his pickup?"

Still no sign of any emotion. "Plenty. But I didn't do it. I wouldn't even know where to look for his brake pipes. Gina would, but I don't think it was her. She'd have got mucked up crawling on the ground under his car, and you'll know when she gets back because there'll be oil and stuff all over her leathers."

I sipped at the weak tea. "You know, Rachel, you're giving me the impression that you don't much care what happens to Frank."

"That's because I don't. You don't know him. You only met the fake Frenchman. I've lived with the real McCoy for yonks and he's not Mr nice guy. If I had any sense, I'd have walked years ago, but..." She shrugged. "I don't know what I'd do if I didn't stick with him, and I don't fancy a life on the dole in Liverpool. I've no family and any friends I had are all over the country by now. He might not be good fun, but he's all I've got."

"If someone does put him out of the way, who gets all this?" I waved at the van and in the general direction of the fair outside."

"I think me and Gina split it seventy-thirty in her favour, but that won't amount to much after the debts have been paid off."

"The fair's in debt?"

"It always owes money. Mostly to the banks. Whenever he squares the loans up, Frank goes out and buys another ride, and he needs another loan to pay for it. Right now, he's paying for the slingshot which he bought second hand and it still cost him the thick end of forty grand. He reckons another two years before it's paid for itself, and a few more before the loan's paid off."

Her argument didn't make complete sense. I'd no doubt she was telling the truth, but the banks were not stupid. They would insist on security, probably in the form of the ride itself, and even so, the loans were probably insured against his death. On personal level, I was glad I'd paid that cheque into the bank. All I had to worry about now was whether the fair's bank would honour it.

Rachel wasn't quite finished. "Listen, missus, you wanna go out there and speak to the crew, be my guest, but I'll tell you now, you'll get nothing out of 'em. Plenty of 'em don't like Frank, some of 'em are okay with him, but fairground folk don't trust townies like you, and even if they did know who cut his brakes, they wouldn't tell you. They'd deal with it their own way."

I got to my feet and prepared to leave. "I

understand, but it's more complicated than that. Cutting his brakes is a criminal offence, the police already know about it and they will pay you a visit."

"And no one'll speak to them either."

Although her opinion was probably accurate, it didn't help much. The police were never too happy with vigilante justice, and I didn't care for it either. I needed these people to talk.

I was about to leave when there was a knock at the door and without waiting for an invitation, a man stepped in.

Aged about thirty, scruffily dressed in denims and a shabby, dirty, white T-shirt, his face was set in a scowl easily matched by Rachel. "Where's dipstick?" he demanded.

"You wanna be careful he don't hear you, Dodds," Rachel warned him. "He had to go out. Problems with the slingshot. Why?"

"Because he's got problems with the dodgems, too. Electrics are playing up, and since he's the expert, he needs to get 'em put right or you'll have a lot of punters demanding their money back tomorrow."

Rachel would not hear it. "You've had this argument with him before, and he warned you the other day, didn't he? You put it right. That's what you get paid for. You and Eddie Zannis, so either get on with it or pack your gear and get out."

"Eddie's out with that tart and I'm on me own, so I'm not doing it. Frank can get stuffed. I'm not risking my neck on that piece of crap. Not while I've no one with me. And if Mr Wonderful wants to argue about it, he knows where he can find me."

And with that, Dodds turned and stormed out.

Rachel's eyes met mine. "See what I mean?"

"Is it like this all the time?"

"All the time. There's a rumour that Willy Dodds is Frank's son, but it's never been proved. Certainly my old man had a thing with Willy's mother thirty years ago, and Willy happened along about nine months later. Frank denies it and Willy goads him. But for all his mouth, Frank's never yet got round to sacking him, and he's been with us since he was a kid."

"What about his mother?"

"Heidi? She runs the hook-a-duck stall for the kids."

"And the other man you spoke of? Zannis, was it?"

"Eddie works with Willy on the dodgems. He's Gina's current flavour of the month."

"Ah. Gina is the tart Dodds was referring to?"

Rachel nodded. "I'm telling you, Mrs sticking-your-nose-in, they're fairground folk. You're wasting your time and money. They won't talk to you and they won't talk to the filth."

"To be accurate, it's your husband's money I'm wasting. He's already paid me."

I heard the sound of a motorcycle pulling up at the adjacent caravan and gave Rachel a 'see you later' nod, before stepping out of the van. There was no problem with Kaiser the dog barking at me. He was already barking at the man who climbed off the rear of the bike, while the rider climbed off, stood the bike on its support and took off her helmet to reveal short cropped, dark hair and a scowl that was a good match for Rachel even though the latter claimed not to be her mother.

Even through the red and black motorcycle leathers, a perfect match for the bike's colour scheme, she looked painfully thin, hair the colour of ebony, and with an angular, bony, face which could have scuttled a thousand ships with one glare from the fiery, green eyes.

I was about to approach and speak to her, when she opened the door to the adjacent van and disappeared inside, slamming it behind her. I chose to concentrate on her boyfriend. "Are you out of favour?"

He let his helmet swing in his hands and gave me a grin. "You could say that. She wanted this pair of rip-knee jeans but didn't have enough dosh and I'm skint, too. Who are you?"

"Christine Capper. Blogger. I'm doing a series on the background to the Wool Fair and I want to feature your efforts. You know. The fairground folk who entertain us Haxforders." He began to walk away as if he were making for another van, and I fell in alongside him. "I just met a man named Willy Dodds. Rachel tells me you and he work the dodgems."

He nodded. "Work being the right word. Hard work. They break down more times than they're worth."

"So Mr Dodds was saying. Apparently there's some kind of problem with the electricity right now."

His craggy features registered concern. "Hell. I'd better get over there. If Frank's there, he'll—"

"Frank's in Bolton. He needed new bungee ropes or something."

"Thank god for that. When he loses it, you've never seen anything like it. Sorry, missus, but I'll have to get over there. If you wanna talk later, you know where to find me."

Chapter Six

Gloomy thoughts were going through my mind on Friday morning. If no one would speak to me or the police, how would we ever learn who was behind the attack on Kilsby? It was all very well people like Sherlock Holmes, Hercule Poirot, and Miss Marple relying on deduction, but you could only make accurate deductions from information and the best source of that information, true or false, was people.

That's not a hard and fast rule. For example, when I saw Dennis gulping down a cup of tea and skipping his usual bowl of Weetabix or Corn Flakes, it was fairly easy to deduce that he intended milking Sandra Limpkin's offer of free breakfast for all it was worth over the coming ten or eleven days. Even so, the deduction came from information: i.e. ingrained knowledge of my husband gleaned over three decades of cohabitation and marriage.

And talking of my husband, he was in a bit of a spat the night before when the remotes wouldn't work. He'd forgotten the batteries, too, but I managed to lay the blame with him, whereupon, he took them back from my pocket recorder and put them back in the handsets.

None of which got me any closer to identifying

Kilsby's attacker.

After posting my weekly vlog (I finished editing it the previous evening) filled with the anticipatory excitement of the Haxford Wool Fair, I rang Kilsby at ten and was told that the 'filth were already on site', and I left the house coming up to half past ten. The sun was shining again, it was pleasantly warm, and I'd abandoned the business suit in favour of the I Luv Blondie t-shirt, tight jeans and comfy trainers. Maybe these people would relate to casual dress rather than the officious businesswoman.

When I got to Barncroft's Meadow I was more than a little peeved to find some autocratic jobsworth charging me five pounds to park the car, despite my repeating several times that I was there on official business.

"So am I, luv." He held out his hand. "Fiver."

In the end I handed over the money and received a ticket from what looked like one of those machines bus conductors used in the days when we had bus conductors.

I wandered towards the fair debating whether or not I could bill Kilsby for the ticket. It was, after all, a legitimate expense. But then, he'd already paid me £400 and he might kick off about it. I would.

I ambled into the fairground which was already open for business, to find Rachel Kilsby in her little booth selling tickets… only she wasn't because she had no customers. When I asked after her husband, she didn't have a clue and had no interest. "Try the slingshot. They're still trying to get it properly rigged."

I turned to walk away only to find a boisterous

collie hurtling towards me and a man running after him shouting "Banjo, Banjo."

The dog jumped up at me and almost landed his front paws on my shoulders, while I looked around for a musician. Then I recognised the man running towards me as George Ibble, one of our best known sheep farmers and a renowned trainer of sheepdogs. His animals had won a pocketful of awards all over the North of England.

"Banjo, come here you little so and so."

At that point I registered the dog's name as Banjo, gave up the search for a wandering minstrel, and ruffled the dog's ears.

"Hello, George."

"Oh, hello, Chrissy. Sorry about this." He slipped a rope leash round Banjo's neck and pulled the dog back to his side. "He's only a pup. Twelve months old. I'm still training him and I'm putting him in the junior obedience show tomorrow afternoon." George's wrinkled features sagged. "Can't see him winning any ribbons for a year or two."

The dog sat at his side, panting, tongue lolling, looking up at me with eyes pleading for food. I stroked his ears again. "Typical teenager, is he?"

"A flaming tearaway. And it's not like he doesn't know his name, but he gets excited when there are people about. I thought I'd bring him here today, get him used to the crowds before the show." He shook his head. "I've got a bad feeling about it."

"I'm sure you'll get him there one day, George." I noticed a familiar figure making notes in a pocketbook as he spoke to Madame Márta, the

Runcorn Romany. "You'll have to excuse me," I said to George. "I'm here on business, too, and I've just seen some of it over there."

Detective Constable Simon Capper was a source of pride to me. When he was coming up to leaving school, Dennis hoped that our son would join him at Haxford Fixers, but Simon decided to forego the dubious pleasure of repairing cars and follow in his mother's footsteps instead. After three years at Leeds University, he joined the police. Six years down the line, he was now part of Haxford's small CID team. As a graduate, he could have asked for fast track promotion, but that would have meant moving to Huddersfield, Bradford, Leeds or Wakefield, and he wanted to stay in his home town. Such a move could come later, when he was through his 'apprenticeship'. He'd waited long enough and the chance came at the beginning of the year when an older officer retired and created wriggle room in the budget. Was he happy? He was overjoyed. He saw the move as the opportunity to make a serious difference to crime levels in Haxford, even if it did entail longer hours.

I stood a discreet distance from him and in a position where he would be sure to notice me, and waited until he was finished with Márta. A few minutes later, he thanked her and joined me.

"Morning, Mam. What are you doing here other than poking your nose in where it doesn't concern you?"

He half bent and I stretched up to peck him on the cheek. "It does concern me, Simon. You're looking into the report your father sent about the brake pipes on Frank Kilsby's pick up, aren't you?"

He tutted. "I didn't know Dad kept you in the loop. He only talks to you about cars and his dinner."

I echoed his tuts. "I got the report off your dad, but I have to ask, doesn't Minx tell you anything? I was with Kilsby when his brakes failed, and he's hired me to find out who's threatening his life. Kilsby's hired me, I mean, not Minx."

Simon chuckled. "Don't let Vic Hillman hear you calling him Minx, and no, I didn't know you were with Kilsby, and I didn't know he'd hired you. When I spoke to him, he did mention something about threats, but to be honest, Mam, I scored him as a bit of a berk. Calls himself Ketchak and talks with a fake French accent. A bit like her." He aimed his pen at Márta's tent. "Reckons she's a genuine Romany born in Budapest, which she thinks is in Rumania when it's in Hungary, and she has an accent that's more like Rochdale."

"Runcorn, so I'm told. Show folk. They don't live in the real world like us." I sighed. "I had to wonder about Kilsby, too, but after what happened, there's something going on."

"Well, you know the script. If you learn anything, you have to let us know."

"Stop worrying. When do I keep secrets from you?"

He laughed again. "Do you want me to write a list? I'll have to get on, Mam. Hey, you remember you and Nam are bringing Beth here tomorrow?"

"Would I forget? You won't be with us?"

He waved around. "Depends how I get on with

this lot. They don't like talking to the filth. Oh, while I think on, I was having a cuppa with Sandra Limpkin about ten minutes ago and she was asking for your number. Has she not rung you?"

"Not yet. I'll go and have a word before I speak to Kilsby."

Forgetting to berate him for calling Naomi 'Nam' and Bethany 'Beth', I left Simon to his work and wandered further through the fair, making for Sandra's van. Even though it was Friday, there were plenty of people about, mainly young women and couples with children or older couples with what I assumed were grandchildren. It would be much busier over the weekend and yet Sandra already had a queue at her van, the tempting aroma of food putting out a call to the forever hungry.

The van was painted a dark maroon, and above the serving area was a banner which read, SANDRA'S SNACKY. GOOD FOOD, LOW PRICES. That it appeared to be printed and pasted onto the van's frame led me to conclude the van belonged to someone else, and Sandra had only borrowed it for the duration of the fair. I recalled Dennis mentioning that she had hired it. Even so, it must have belonged to a catering outfit of some kind because it was fitted out with all the necessary equipment for a fast food stall.

She was getting through the queue at breakneck speed, almost throwing the burgers, buns, cups of tea in plastic cups at her customers, and raking in a small fortune. Her sister Alice was working alongside Sandra, and in the background was her teenage son, Tommy, a gormless nineteen-year-old, reminiscent of Nick Kilsby (according to Frank). Tommy's IQ registered somewhere slightly lower than Cappy the Cat's or maybe even George Ibble's dog, Banjo. At least, that was my experience of him. He was a college student (though I couldn't imagine what he might be studying) and Sandra had never entertained the idea of employing him at the mill. "He'd burn the place down in a morning," she had once told me. Instead, she employed her daughter, Ulrika for the mill's Snacky.

As I arrived, George Ibble took Banjo off to one side and fed him a sausage roll in bits. As he fed him each morsel, he spoke to the dog. I didn't think sausage rolls were on the approved list of dogs' dietary requirements, but it seemed to be working. Banjo's attention was riveted on George... and the rest of the sausage roll.

Sandra spotted me, had a quiet word with Alice, and then motioned me to come to the rear of the van. As I made my way round, I passed three large gas bottles and a small generator, and the thought crossed my mind: keep Dennis away. He'd have that generator in bits to find out what it tick.

I got to the back of the stall and Sandra emerged from the rear door and descended short flight of steps to join me. Alongside the steps was a stack of inverted bread trays, on top of which stood a couple of trays of buns.

She knew how to mince fresh beef but she didn't mince her words. Sandra was WYSIWYG. Upset her and the beans on toast would likely end up as beans on head... your head. Dennis would hear no wrong said against her. As far as he was concerned, the sun shone out of her bacon and egg double deckers, and on those occasions when I'd called there, I'd always found her chatty and cheerful. But then I'd never caught her in a bad mood.

Until now.

A usually cheerful, chubby, blonde-haired, fifty year old – give or take – she was anything but smiles when she greeted me. "I am fed-fizzing-up. Do you know how much this mob are charging me for this pitch?"

"A pretty penny, I'll bet."

"It's robbery without violence. What with the cost of stock and the rent, hire of the van and gas bottles, most of what I'll take through the day will go straight to suppliers and these thieving toe rags, Kilsby and his crew."

"Evenings and weekends are traditionally busiest at the Wool Fair, though," I said.

"Aye, and I'll need it. By the time I'm done, I'll be making less per day than I was twenty years ago. And I wouldn't care but the council on Kilsby's behalf after he asked them to recommend a good caterer. I never asked for it."

That was out of character for Haxford Borough Council. "How come they came to you? I mean, you don't usually do site catering."

"Ellen Plymstock fell ill. This is her van." Sandra waved at the snack bar. "Her and her old man usually stand the Wool Fair, but she had a wobbler the other week."

"Heart attack?"

Sandra nodded. "So they reckon. She's only about fifty-five, an'all. Makes you wonder, Chrissy.

You're about that age, aren't you?"

Thanks for that, Sandra, I thought. "What? And Charlie couldn't manage on his own?"

"He has to be at home to look after her. Promised me he'd do me a deal on hiring his van, and he did; a deal in his favour. I'm sure I could have bought one cheaper. And even then I had to get your Cappy and Grimy to tow it here."

"He told me about the deal. I'll be honest, Sandra, the way Dennis eats, it might have been cheaper to ask him for a bill rather than feed him and his mates for a week." A question occurred to me. "If you and Alice are working here, who's manning the Snacky at the mill?"

"Our Ulrika. Her and a couple of casuals I use now and then."

The opening skirmishes were done with and it was time to get down to business. "You asked our Simon for my number."

"Oh. Right. Yeah. Fact is, I need your help, Chrissy."

"I shouldn't think I can tell you anything about catering, Sandra."

"Not about flaming catering. You're a private investigationator, aren't you?"

Like many a Haxforder, Sandra spoke only two languages: bad and bad English. "A private investigator? Yes. You know I am. You speak to Dennis often enough."

"Well I need you to private investigate."

"Investigate what?"

"Some thieving toe rag is nicking me buns."

There were so many possible answers to that,

most of them ribald and unrepeatable, that I had to force myself not to laugh. "Run that by me again, luv."

"You heard. Some rotten tea leaf is having it away with my buns while my back's turned. Crikey, our Tommy only picked them up half an hour ago and three buns have gone missing off the tray already." She hastened on to explain the situation. "I can't keep up with the baking out here, so Ulrika's doing them for me at the mill, and when they're ready, I send Tommy over to pick them up. But I can't sell 'em while they're hot, so I leave 'em out here on the tray until they cool off." She gestured at the upturned bread trays and the cooling buns. "Some rotten tealeaf has had it away with them… well, three of them anyway. I just need you to point him out and I'll give him a pasting, cos it's gotta be some kid."

Sandra obviously thought I was still working as an amateur. Considering the amount of time she spent speaking to Dennis and his partners, I thought she'd have been more aware of my calling. "And you want to hire me?"

"Well, I can hardly bell the filth, can I? Can you imagine how your Simon would react if I called him in?"

I could imagine all right. "I'm not trying to put you off, Sandra, but do you know much I charge?"

"Can't be more than few quid for a job like this, can it?"

"Twenty pounds… an hour… plus expenses."

"How much? Hell's bells. And I thought the gas companies were ripping us off."

You should see how much other detective agencies charge. That's what I wanted to say, but I didn't. Instead, I made the effort to calm her down. "Take it easy, Sandra, or you'll end up in the next bed to Ellen Plymstock. I'm sure we can come to some arrangement. For instance, would you consider sponsoring one of my vlogs? I can do you a deal on that which will only cost you forty or fifty pounds, but even so, I can only give you a limited amount of time looking for your bun thief."

"I'll give it a coat of thinking about."

"Good, and in the meantime, I'll keep my eyes open."

It was the kind of promise I could make without committing to anything too demanding. I had more on my plate than hanging around the rear of her van keeping an eye on two trays of buns. The logical approach would be to have Ulrika bake them the night before and put them on the counter where she could keep an eye on them, but I could see that if she ran out she would need fresh from the mill, and she would still face the same issue of cooling them off. It was not an insurmountable problem but one which needed better organisation than she was employing.

As far as the threat to Frank Kilsby was concerned, I was making zero progress, and I decided it was time to get on with it. I needed to know who, amongst his crew, would know where, how and when to get at his brake lines. Not only that, but they would have to be quick. If Kilsby was right – and I no longer had any cause to doubt him – those lines were cut while he was parked outside the

Haxford Arms, in broad daylight on one of the busiest roads in and out of Haxford.

I was about to make for the slingshot when I spotted Simon again at the .22 shooting gallery, and his conversation with the proprietor/operator didn't look too friendly. The man behind the counter, a balding fifty-year-old was gesticulating wildly, arms waving here and there while the occasional finger pointed at Simon, at his rifles, or into thin air.

Intrigued – all right, nosy – I ambled across until I came within earshot, and staying out of Simon's eye line, listened in on the conversation. It did not make for pleasant listening.

"I'm telling you, pal, it was there first thing."

Simon made an effort to placate the stallholder. "Mr Singer—"

Singer waved behind him. "Six targets." He gestured at the counter. "Six rifles. Only there aren't six. There's only five. Someone has pinched one of me guns."

Fairgrounds, I knew, were hotbeds of theft, but it was usually pickpockets or bag-snatchers. But on a level of seriousness and taking into account the threats made against Kilsby, a stolen rifle was way more worrying than three buns missing from Sandra's snack van.

I heard the stall holder complaining. "Do you know how much it costs me to stand here? And now I'm not only a rifle down, but someone's actually nicked the thing. I'm losing money left, right, and centre."

"They're chained to the counter," Simon argued as I edged closer.

Singer held up a rifle-less chain at the far end of the stall. "They snipped the end off the chain, didn't they?"

Even from my poor vantage point, I could see what he meant. The chains were anchored to the counter on split rings, like a key ring. At the other end, the BB guns were fastened by a similar split ring set into bottom edge of the rifle stock, but the chain without a rifle had been cut one or two links further back.

I made my presence known. "I'm sorry, Simon, but I couldn't help overhearing."

My son vented his spleen on me. "And even if you could help it, you wouldn't. Just go about your business, Mam, I'll deal with this."

"Yes, but I'm thinking of that business with Mr Kilsby's pickup yesterday. I mean, if this gentleman has lost a rifle—"

"It's a BB gun, Mam, not an SA80." I was wondering what an SA80 was when Simon went on. "He's not gonna get his head blown off with…"

Simon trailed off at the sound of a woman and two children running from the ghost train and screaming, "He's dead, he's dead, he's dead."

Singer turned pale. In better control of ourselves, Simon and I hurried across to the woman who was hugging her two yawping children to her legs.

"It's okay, luv," Simon soothed her. "Take it easy."

"He's dead," she cried.

"Listen to my son," I urged. "He's a police officer. Now, who's dead?"

She waved a frantic arm at the ghost train. "In

there. The carriage hit him and he's dead."

I could see the doubt written in my son's face. The ghost train was designed to scare, and there were any number of ways in which they could set up the illusion of the car hitting someone. On the other hand, they had run out of the attraction on foot. Well, they would, wouldn't they? It would be difficult to run out on hands and knees. Assuming they went in aboard a car, where was it?

Young Nick was at the station where riders boarded the cars, but nothing was moving and there was no one manning the control booth. Nick stared helplessly around while the punters whined at him.

Simon was in his element. "I'll check it out, Mam. Can you look after them?" He gestured at the distressed woman and her children.

"Of course."

Before he could move, another young woman emerged from the tunnel and I recognised her as Gina. Maybe Simon's age (twenty-seven) she was about my height, her black hair dishevelled, a range of tattoos on her arms, which had been hidden by the motorcycle leathers when I last saw her, but which now gave the impression that she had not washed. The most striking thing about her was her green eyes; yesterday they were forbidding. Now they were sunken, hollow, shocked.

"It's my dad. Frank. One of the cars hit him and I think he's dead."

Chapter Seven

Simon went into the ghost train via the exit. Still distressed, the first woman grabbed her two children by the hand, and made for the fairground exit, despite my protesting that the police would need a statement from her. "They can do the other," she shouted over her shoulder.

It left me alone with Gina, but soon after Simon disappeared, other customers emerged from the right hand end, where the cars went in, and like the young mother and her children, they were on foot. They were puzzled and annoyed, muttering between themselves, and the queue which was waiting to take the ride began to disperse, leaving Nick completely flummoxed..

My heart sank and I questioned Gina. "Are you sure he's dead?" I asked.

She nodded. "You don't know how much those cars weigh. They're not fast, but it looks like it's knocked him flat and then bumped up onto him. I'd better tell Rache." She was about to move on when she stopped herself and her eyes narrowed on me. "You were talking to Eddie yesterday. Just who are you?"

"Christine Capper. Technically, I'm a blogger and vlogger, but your father hired me to find out who was threatening him."

"Ah. You're the nosy parker, are you? I should have guessed when you were talking to my fella."

"Yes. I am. And yesterday, I wasn't sure that I believed your dad. Obviously, I was wrong, and I take that personally." I realised how bitter I sounded and tried to make amends. "I, er, I'm sorry for your loss, Gina, but I will make it my business to find the culprit."

She scowled. "Well, let's hope you make a better job of it than you have done so far." And with that she stomped off towards the ticket booth and her stepmother.

Ignorance, arrogance like that usually rattled me into a response, but I made allowances for her. She'd just found her father dead in the complex of tunnels behind the spooky façade.

At this point, I realised that both Gina and I were jumping to conclusions. He'd been threatened, yes, but there was nothing to suggest that this was murder. He'd been hit by one of the cars, Gina said. What was he doing on the track was my first question, and then I recalled him saying that he was instrumental in the setup because he was the only person who knew how it all went together. If anyone had the right to be on that track, it was him, and that led to the next question. Had something gone wrong, something which needed his attention? It must have, or why was he in there?

No matter what the circumstances, the Haxford grapevine would not take long to spread the word and I knew that within the next quarter of an hour, he would be the victim of a mafia hit or Yorkshire witchcraft and there would be a crowd of ghouls hovering round the ghost train. When it came to spreading the word, social media couldn't hold a candle to the gossips of Haxford.

With no sign of Simon coming out, I took a walk around the ride. It was much larger than I imagined. When you come across these things on fairgrounds, you see the front, with its scary scenes above the entrance, and in this case, it had wings built on each end of the façade so you couldn't see past them without actually cutting through the gap between the ghost train and the waltzer on one side or Madame Márta's place on the other.

When I cut through that narrow alley, I realised that it was as large as the dodgems, the main difference being that this was a solid construction, large, wooden boards, painted black (on both sides, I assumed) and no windows. They would be counterproductive, wouldn't they? The ghost train travelled in darkness with the creepy exhibits floodlit or backlit. At the rear, the ground was littered with heavy duty cables, straggling wormlike across the grass and leading back to a large van which held the generator. That was one for Dennis who would no doubt be able to tell me how it worked, how much power it generated, the diameter of the cables required to carry that power, and their scrap metal value.

I noticed that there was no sign of an access door. It seemed, then, that the only way in was through the official 'station' as they called the place where punters got into the cars.

And then I found it. It wasn't a proper door, and

the seal between it and adjacent panels was so tight that it could easily be missed. It was obviously designed to ensure that not a single crack of light shone through from the outside, and to that end, there was no door handle, only a square slot where you would insert a matching T-bar and twist to gain access.

Kilsby was the main man, but there must be other crew members who knew what they were doing with the ghost train, and if his death was suspicious in any way, or even if it wasn't, they were the ones I (and the police) would need to question.

Behind the generator van, was a patch of open grass which led down to the river's edge, and I followed it until I reached the trees lining the shallow banks of the Hax, then looked to my right. I was fifty yards from the nearest of the accommodation caravans.

I made my way back to the front of the train, and as I got there, Simon emerged from the exit, his mobile glued to his ear.

"Just giving Mandy Hiscoe the full SP," he told me as he ended the call. "Too dark to see properly in there, so she's sending a couple of forensic men down and the doc. We'll know more when they get him out."

"Suspicious?" I asked, my little journey into the nether world of the fairground preying on my mind.

"Doesn't look like it. He must have been working in there and tripped or something, and fallen across the track and the car's come round and hit him. Definitely dead, though."

When it came to emotions I was better than Mr Spock at keeping them under control. I had to be. I was a professional private eye, a former police officer. We didn't break down on the job. We had to be strong. All the same, when I tried to analyse my feelings, I found a tumult of different emotions juggling for top spot: anger, chagrin, and some sadness. No matter what he thought of himself, Frank Kilsby was not an attractive man and if his wife was to be believed, he was not a particularly nice man, but whether by accident or design, he did not deserve to die like this. No one did.

"You get off home, Mam. This ride'll be shut for the rest of the day and there's nothing you can do about his cut brake pipes, is there?"

"He paid me to find the man who threatened him, Simon, and I find it too coincidental that, twenty-four hours later, he's dead. I'll carry on asking my questions if you don't mind."

"Or even if I do mind. It's up to you. But don't forget if you do learn anything, you must let us know." He looked across at the ticket booth where a queue was forming because Gina was talking to her stepmother. "Right now, I need a word with her, see if there's any proper lighting in there and get it switched on."

"Yes. I need a word with her too."

A few minutes later we were with the two women who, between arguing with the queue waiting for tickets, were deep in irritated conversation. Gina regarded us both with suspicion, Rachel with complete disinterest, and while we spoke with her stepdaughter, she got on with the business of selling tickets.

Simon took the lead. "I can hardly see anything in there, miss. Is there any proper lighting?"

"Nope."

"So how do they go on when they have to do repairs and what have you?"

"They use flashlights. Don't you have them in this part of the world?"

I could see Simon was struggling to hold his temper. "Right, well the ride's shut for now until our people get here. I don't know when you'll be allowed to open up again, and I'm sorry, but I don't know how long it'll be before they get your father's body out of there."

"Whatever."

Gina was about to go back to haggling with her stepmother, when I stopped her. "Just a minute. What was Frank doing in there?"

"Checking a complaint."

"What complaint?"

"Why don't you mind your own business?"

"Your father paid me not to."

"Well—"

Simon cut in on her. "You'll answer Mrs Capper, Ms Kilsby, or I'll ask the same question and you'll have to answer me."

She let out an exasperated sigh and when she spoke it was to Simon, not me. "Some whinger came out moaning that the Dracula puppet had almost fallen on him. I couldn't leave the control station, Nick doesn't have the brains to handle it, so I rang my old man and he came over to deal with it. It happens. Right? They spend two days putting the ride up and they make mistakes, and if our old fella found out who'd done it, he'd have knuckled him. That's it. That's what he was doing in there."

Simon might have let it go at that, but I wouldn't. "So why wasn't the ride stopped until he was finished?"

"Cos he told me not to. Listen, missus nosy nose, he was the bees' knees with that thing, my dad. He knew every square inch of the layout. He knew where, when and how to get out of the way of the cars and he knew how big a gap there was between them. I don't know what went wrong. Maybe he tripped or something, banged his head when he fell and while he was half out of it, the car came round and smashed him. Right? Is that it? Can I go now?"

"One thing," I insisted. "How big a gap is there between cars?"

Gina shrugged. "Search me. About half a minute or something. Maybe less, maybe more. I don't know, cos I've never timed it." And with that, she strode off.

Simon smiled indulgence on me. "You don't let go, do you, Mam?"

"And you'll soon learn not to, luv."

He wandered off to try dispersing the crowd now gathering outside the ghost train. Waste of time. If I knew anything about my fellow Haxforders, this would be a bigger attraction than anything the Wool Fair had to offer. I decided I needed another cup of tea, and strolled over to Sandra's van, only to find a huge queue waiting for service, and Sandra apparently AWOL. I could see the rear door was open so I walked round the back and found her picking up the bun tray.

"Two more gone missing," she shouted. "At this rate, I'll have none left by dinner time. I've had to ring Ulrika and tell her to put fresh in the oven and let them cool off there before I send Tommy to collect them. I thought you were gonna—"

I cut her off. "I'm sorry, Sandra, but I can't stand guard here all the time. If that's what you're asking, you need a security guard not a private eye." I backed off a little. "You've heard the news, I suppose?"

"Aye. Ketchup's dead so they say."

"He is. And his name is Ketchak... well, actually, it's Kilsby, but let's not split hairs."

"I know. The minute I met him I sussed him. About as French as Yorkshire pudding. Still, the chances are it'll drag every banana in Haxford here and I'll make fortune... but not on me buns." She, too, cooled off a little. "Was there something you wanted, or were you checking on the buns?"

I dug into my purse, handed over a pound and said, "I could do with a cuppa. No sugar."

She ignored the offer of money. "On the house. Wait there."

Sandra's van backed onto the open spaces of the meadow, and further up the field, not far from the roped off enclosures for the various livestock shows, I could see George Ibble working with Banjo. I couldn't hear him for the noise of the fairground, but I guessed he was giving the dog commands, and Banjo was obeying... when he felt like it. He responded to the orders when they were verbal, but the visual commands appeared to remain a mystery to him. When George threw out his left arm, Banjo cocked his head one side and then lay down, tail wagging, waiting for the next order. I didn't hear what it was, but Banjo turned, dashed towards a clutch of bushes on the right, sniffed for suitable spot, and then squat, in response to which, George pushed back his cap, and shook his head. Moments later, Banjo came back, tail wagging, pleased that he had relieved himself of the burden, and sat at George's feet, while the master, with much finger-pointing, spoke to him.

Patience, George, I said to myself. And patience was what I needed. Simon might not accept Kilsby's death as murder, but I didn't like coincidences and coming on the back of his severed brake pipes, I was convinced that his death was anything but accidental. More than that, Gina said her father knew every inch of the train's interior. In that case, what did he trip over? She said he and his crew made use of flashlights when they were working on the interior. Surely he would have one lit while he was making his way to the faulty exhibit. I was certain that something else had happened, something which brought him down in the path of the car, but for now, I couldn't imagine what.

Sandra came back with a cup of tea and we spent another few minutes chatting while I drank it off, and then I made my way back to the ghost train where, as I anticipated, Simon had failed in his attempt at getting the crowds to clear off, but at least he had help now in the shape of a few uniforms. They had already taped off the ghost train as a crime scene, and I also noticed two men, both fairground workers by the look of them, lifting up sections of the roof.

"Getting some natural light in," my son told me when I asked. He was busy pulling on a forensic suit, and I saw a couple of CSI people doing the same, and the pathologist, already swathed in his sterile suit and overshoes, waiting to go in. "I have to show them the way," Simon reported, and then smiled on me. "Why are you still here, Mam?"

"I told you, Simon, this is not an accident."

"Nothing to say otherwise yet," he said. "But ten to one, Mandy will want a full statement off you."

"I already gave one to Minx."

"She'll want another." He laughed. "And don't call him Minx. He'll take it out on me."

"Well, if he does, let me know. I'll put him in his place." One of the forensic men gave Simon the thumbs up. "It looks like you're on."

"I'll catch you later."

And I'll be waiting here, I thought as he led the small team into the attraction.

I guessed it would be a long wait. The doctor would carry out an initial assessment in situ but he was unlikely to come to any conclusions until a full post mortem took place, and even then he would probably conclude crush injuries from collision with the car. Anticipating that situation, I wouldn't argue with it. My concern was the cause of his fall into the path of the cars.

Right then I would love to have been stationed in a helicopter, or better yet, one of those cradles you see when engineers work on street lamps. Anything to lift me from the ground and let me look down into the now roofless ghost train and see what was going on.

I knew, of course. Simon would be standing by waiting for news, the doctor would be crouched over the body and the forensic officers would be taking photographs prior to mounting their search for tiny fragments of evidence. So, yes, I knew, but I would love to have been up there watching.

Half an hour passed. A grumble in my tummy told me I was due for some lunch but I could not leave. Not until I knew.

And then Simon reappeared. He had removed his facemask and he was talking on the phone, his features grim, and in that moment I knew I had got it right.

He confirmed it. "Nasty bruise on his temple which the doc couldn't account for until one of the forensic men found a BB pellet nearby. Looks like someone shot at him, it hit the side of his head and he keeled over right in front of the oncoming car."

Chapter Eight

Mandy Hiscoe's bump was impossible to hide, but with her usual air of laissez faire, she didn't care. I knew her well, and I knew she would go on working until she went into labour. A bubbly blonde, unmarried by choice, she was a hard-working detective, with a fine clear up rate, to which she could add the Graveyard Poisoner. She was with me the day we cracked the case.

Haxford's comparatively low levels of crime, both in terms of number and severity, meant that local CID did not warrant the presence of an inspector or above on permanent station. Mandy was, therefore, the senior officer, and reported to DI Quinn who was based in Huddersfield. It was the best place for him as far as I was concerned, although if it were within my power I'd be tempted to transfer him to the Shetlands or Orkneys, whichever was the coldest and most uncomfortable. I would even suggest The Falklands, but I wasn't sure whether they employed British police officers.

Mandy was as chalk to Quinn's cheese. Where he was scathing, especially when dealing with me, Mandy was patient, and although she could be tough when she was pressing a suspect, she maintained the underlying principle of law:

innocent until proven guilty. Quinn on the other hand, was always in a hurry. If I'd had him taking my statement, he would have dismissed the note Kilsby received and the deliberately ruptured brake lines to concentrate on the man's death in the ghost train. Mandy didn't. Sat in her car, she wanted to know everything from the moment Kilsby first rang me.

When I was through, she spent a moment re-reading my statement, her brow creased. "What I find odd, Chrissy, is that Hillman only took a statement from Kilsby after the accident outside the station yesterday. He didn't take one from you."

"He wouldn't, would he? He doesn't like me. He never did, and he'd be scared I was trying to steal his thunder. He wasn't interested, Mandy. He was too determined to prove that Kilsby was drunk. Trivia like the bits and pieces I might have known didn't figure in his thinking."

"I'll have a word. Won't do much good, I don't think. He outranks me in terms of service, but I'll shout at him for you. Now, you were here yesterday, you've been here this morning. You've obviously spoken to people. Any leads?"

"None... well, maybe, but nothing concrete. Neither the wife, Rachel, nor the daughter, Gina, appeared particularly upset by his death, and neither of them has a seriously good word to say about him. Kilsby himself admitted that he was a bit of a dictator. He didn't court popularity and from what he and Rachel told me, he didn't have a large crowd of friends. After his immediate family, you could have an army of suspects."

"And he couldn't narrow it down for you?"

"No. I imagine that if he had any idea, he'd have dealt with the matter rather than ringing me. He came across as that kind of man."

Mandy shuffled through the various scraps of paper on her knee. "According to Simon, there's a BB air rifle missing from the shooting gallery. That's got to be the weapon."

"I'd agree, but the stallholder, a man named Singer, was giving Simon some grief over it. It was as if he'd reported it rather than Simon questioning him."

"I'd better get a statement from him. The weapon hasn't been found."

"Try the river," I suggested, and when her eyebrows rose, I explained what I'd seen on my excursion behind the ghost train. "The Hax isn't particularly deep there, Mandy, but if someone shot him and left him to be hit by the car, they could have got out through the rear access, hurried over to the bushes by the river, and thrown it in."

"It's still deep enough to wipe out any forensic," she complained. "I'll get someone to search the area. All right, Chrissy. We'll leave it at that, no point telling you to mind your own business, I suppose?"

"None at all. He paid me to find out who was threatening him. I failed. I take it personally." I reached for the door handle. "Have you spoken to Rachel, yet?"

"Your Simon should be interviewing her right now."

"Well, when he's done with her, I'll be speaking

to her."

Mandy wagged a warning finger at me. "Be careful, Chrissy. This is a police matter now."

"And you'll be the first to know anything I learn, and at least I'm dealing with you, not Paddy Quinn."

She laughed. "But not for long." She laughed again when she saw my features cloud over. "Doesn't matter whether it's murder or manslaughter, the minute Paddy gets my report, he'll come flying down here like an extra from a Dirty Harry movie."

My heart sank. "And when he knows I'm on the case, he'll threaten me with Armageddon if I don't back off."

I climbed out of the car and made my way back to the fairground where I headed straight to the ticket booth, only to find that Rachel had handed over to someone else who told me she was in her caravan with the police.

As I headed in that direction, my phone rang. It was Dennis.

"Hey up, lass, what's this I'm hearing about that Killjoy bloke snuffing it?"

"You mean Kilsby."

"Whatever he wants to call himself."

"How did you get to know about it?" I asked.

"Ulrika at the Snacky. Apparently Sandra rang her to order more buns and she told Ulrika that this bloke's been snuffed. Blown away with a machine gun. Is that right?"

I swear that if the government ever wanted to know who was giving away the country's secrets they should look at Haxford first. And as for Chinese whispers... If some man wolf whistled me in the street, by the time Dennis got to know, that stranger and I would have been encamped in an upmarket bachelor pad for an afternoon of rampant fornication. Not that men ever wolf-whistled me in the street. Not these days, anyway.

"He's dead, Dennis, and right now we don't know whether it was an accident or murder. All right?" Okay, so it wasn't the truth, but it might help put the rumours to sleep.

Dennis's reaction surprised me. "Well, that drops me right in it, dunnit?"

"Why? What business is it of yours?"

"I've got his truck here haven't I? And I've done the repair work. He owes me eighty quid, and if he wants me to deliver it, it'll be a ton, and it don't look like he's a position to poppy up, does it?"

"Send the bill to his wife... I mean widow."

"Oh, yeah, and if the fair moves before she pays, how am I gonna find 'em? Well, I'll tell you this much, she won't get the truck back until I get my money, and if they don't pay up, I'll sell it."

"Good. I'll tell her that when I speak to her. Is that all, Dennis? Can I go now?"

My tone of voice was sufficient for Dennis to take the hint and he rang off.

I had barely paused in my stride while talking to him, and as I turned towards the accommodation vans, Simon came out of Rachel's.

"You won't get much change there, Mam."

"You never know, luv. I don't have to worry about things like PACE so I can ask questions you're not allowed to. And don't get your boxer shorts in a knot. I've already told Mandy I'll let her know if I learn anything."

The German shepherd growled and bared his teeth as I approached. "Shut up, Kaiser," I ordered, and to my surprise, he did. Whether it was the tone of voice, the same one I used to put Dennis off, or that he recognised me, I don't know, but he was sullen and quiet long enough for me to knock on the van door.

Rachel opened the door. "Get lost."

Like all caravans, the door opened outwards, and before she could close it again, I grabbed hold of it. "Just a minute, Rachel you need to talk to me."

She looked down at Kaiser whose ears pricked up. "Want me to set the dog on you? One word of command and he'll tear you to pieces."

I took out my smartphone. "One word to my son, and the police will throw you in a cell for killing Frank."

"It wasn't me."

"Right now, you and your stepdaughter are the only two in the frame. Talk to me, Rachel, and let me help prove you didn't kill him."

"I said—"

"I heard you, but that means nothing. Any of you could have sneaked into the ghost train through the rear access, shot Frank, dumped the rifle, and gone about your business leaving it to the car to kill him."

"I was in the ticket booth all morning."

"And you didn't even leave to go to the toilet?"

"Let her in, Rache. It can't do any harm."

The voice from inside the van sent a shiver through me, and for a horrible moment, I thought everyone had got it wrong. It wasn't Kilsby in the ghost train. It was dark in there. Gina could have made a mistake. It wasn't Frank Kilsby but someone else. After all, none of the Haxford police had seen him, other than Minx and the uniforms helping on traffic control, that is, and they were not at the fair. I could have identified him, or not as the case may be, but I didn't go into the ghost train either.

Common sense took over. An hour or longer had passed since his body was brought out, and it was reasonable to assume that Rachel, Gina, other members of the fairground crew had seen him. More than enough for an informal identification.

In that case, who did the disembodied voice belong to?

Rachel stood back to let me in and I entered the van to find Ossie Travis, my dreamboat of the previous day, slipping his muscular arms through the sleeve holes of his black vest, dragging it over his head and letting it down to cover his six-pack. He gave me a salacious grin and made no effort to hide his actions as he fastened the zipper of his jeans.

"How are you, Miss Marbles? Cracked the case yet?"

I couldn't decide whether I was angry or jealous. Surely not the latter? What did this youngish stud have that I didn't have in the shape of my husband? I shifted my concentration as the list began to grow in my head, and answered his insouciant challenge.

"Yes, I've solved it. A wife and her lover determined to get Kilsby out of the way." I took out my phone. "Want me to call the cops now?"

Rachel speared me with glances of pure ice, but Ossie found it funny. "Lovers? Me and Rache? Naw. She was just helping me try on a new thong. I'm thinking of becoming a male stripper."

And I'd pay to see the act.

Once again, I had to take conscious control of my thought processes. Perhaps it was time to insist Dennis give some attention to me instead of his Morris Marina. Then again, maybe not. I'd never forgotten the time he shouted 'chequered flag' while he was in the ultimate throes of satisfaction. If he was going to compare me to anything, I'd rather it was not Brands Hatch.

I concentrated on Rachel. "Your husband's death?"

"Nothing to do with me."

Ossie echoed her statement. "Nor me."

"Neither of you look particularly distressed."

Rachel looked away, then moved to the sink where she filled the kettle plugged it in and got three beakers ready, leaving the challenge to Ossie.

"Distressed? No. Upset, yes. Frank's death throws some large spanners in the works, and we have to work out solutions to the problems it's caused. Will we miss him? Yes. He was a bully, a pain in the butt, but he knew how to make this thing work." He gestured around and I guessed that 'this thing' was the funfair not the caravan. "He could negotiate for the United Nations, and he always screwed the price down to the bottom when haggling for the site rent. He told me back in January that your local council was one of the toughest he'd ever dealt with, but he still got them down by twenty percent." Ossie laughed. "Mind, you Yorkies are all the same, aren't you? Tight to the last pound."

"Don't be so generous," I responded. "We're tight to the last fifty pence." He laughed again and I pressed on. "So he was the big mover and shaker. Who takes it on now?"

"Me, I suppose," Ossie said, accepting a beaker of tea from Rachel. "I've always been his 2IC."

"In his wife's eyes, too." I also took a beaker from her, and gave her a withering glance.

"Disapproval, huh? Very middle class," Ossie commented, and followed it with another surprise. "He knew about us."

"I... What... Oh... He knew?"

"He'd have to be blind, deaf, and stupid not to," Rachel said, cradling her beaker and taking a seat under the window. "Everyone on the site knows. Privacy is a luxury we don't have when we're touring, and unlike you well off townies, we can't afford to book into hotels for the odd quickie."

"Well off? My husband is a mechanic, not an executive." The words reminded me of my conversation with Dennis. "And talking of Dennis, someone owes him about a hundred pounds for the work he did on Frank's pickup truck."

"Tell him to bring it back and we'll pay him," Ossie said. "We're not crooks, Mrs Capper. We pay our way."

"I'll see to it." I sipped the cheap tea. "For now,

if I eliminate you two, and I don't see why I should, but if I do, who's in the frame?"

Rachel shrugged. "You want a list? Start with Dodds and Zannis on the dodgems, then get round to Jim Singer on the shooting gallery – the filth reckon it was one of his rifles – and while you're at it, speak to Dodds's mother, Heidi, and don't forget Mystic Márta. Frank has been giving her the benefit of his horizontal experience for long enough, but he wouldn't throw me out for her. Then there's Pauline on the teacups and helter-skelter, and Kath on the darts. He's had his way with them all."

I was beginning to flounder under the flood of information. "A busy man."

"Why do you think I suspected he'd given you one when I first met you?"

I brimmed with sarcasm. "Yes, well, I'm far too middle class for a bit of rough and tumble just to secure a contract. What about Gina? Would she be glad to see the back of him?"

Rachel shook her head. "No way. I mean I don't think she gave two figs for him, but there's no way she'd waste him."

"You sound very certain of that."

"She's not my daughter but I know her."

"All right. I mentioned contracts, and Frank paid me four hundred pounds to point the finger. If you want me out of your hair, I can work out the actual figure and repay the difference."

"Can you crack it? Are you good enough?"

"Have you ever heard of PACE?"

Ossie nodded. "Police and Criminal Evidence Act."

"Correct. It places restrictions on what the police can and can't do, what they can and can't ask. I used to be a police officer so I know what I'm talking about. As a private investigator, I can ignore it, and you should have guessed that I won't go away."

"But you're hand in glove with the plod," Rachel objected.

"No. My son is a detective constable, and I know most of the police in Haxford, but they won't tell me anything. Frank paid me for two days work. I won't bill you extra, but if you're happy for me to go on, I will."

They exchanged a glance and Ossie spoke for both of them. "Keep the dosh and do whatever you like, but I wouldn't bet on you being able to finger the culprit. If you do get any grief from the crew, refer them to me."

"I'll do that. In the meantime, there's something I could do with from you."

He laughed yet again. "Sorry, girl, Rachel's drained me already."

That remark brought another disapproving stare from me. "Yes. Very funny, Mr Travis. What I need is a plan of the ghost train and I need to know exactly where Frank was found."

"It'll take me a while. Say twenty minutes. I'll have to dig it out of Frank's records, then scan it and print it out, and I'll need to check with Gina. She's knows where he was when she found him. Can you come back?"

"Half an hour," I promised.

Chapter Nine

I came out of the van and as on the previous day, my grumbling tummy told me it had to be lunchtime. As I made my way to Sandra's van I rang Dennis and told him to bring the pickup to the fairground.

"Give me a ring and I'll take you to Kilsby's van and his widow will pay you, but listen to me, Dennis. Make it official. They'll want an invoice."

"Tsk. When do I ever do anything and not put it through the books?"

"Plenty of times, and I'm not sure I can count that far." Before he could respond to my elliptical insult, I asked, "Will you need me to take you back to the mill?"

"No. I'd have to change out of me overalls to ride in your car. I'll get Geronimo to follow me in the van. We'll be there in twenty minutes."

"You'll probably find me at Sandra's snack van."

"Eating again? I thought you were watching your weight."

"It's called lunch, Dennis. The thing that stops you fainting between breakfast and teatime. And unlike you, I'll have to pay for it." With that, I cut the call.

Watching my weight indeed. I didn't really have weight problems. True, I gained a few pounds now and then, usually at times like Christmas and Easter (which was just behind us and the very reason Dennis mentioned it) when I tended to indulge my appetite for cream cakes and chocolate, but most of the time I ate sensibly and kept myself in trim. And I needed to keep on top of such minor weight problems that I had. My brother's daughter, Jocelyn, was marrying in August, and it was a top class, formal do, so I would have to be properly kitted out.

It wasn't a problem for Dennis. He could eat for England but his job kept him active and he burned the calories off quite naturally.

I couldn't say the same for his attitude to Jocelyn's wedding. It was to be held at Gaven Hall near Cambridge, and aside from having to drive us down there and pay for a room, he would have to abandon his overalls and toolbox for an entire weekend. To him it would be like going cold turkey, and I just knew he'd be suffering withdrawal symptoms before we got the other side of Huddersfield.

Sandra was sympathetic when I told her. "They're all the same, fellas. If you can't eat it, play with it, or give it a good seeing to, they don't wanna know. That's why I chose to do without when that one of mine took a hike."

It was an opinion which reminded me of Cappy the Cat as much as it did Dennis, but I wish she hadn't mentioned giving it, 'a good seeing to'. It prompted my vivid imagination to centre on Adonis

Ossie again. *Oh, grow up, woman*, I mentally chastised myself.

Taking a break, leaving the queue to her sister and son, Sandra joined me at the rear of the van, handed me a cheese and tomato sandwich and a plastic cup of decent tea, and asked, "So what's the score with the boss man?"

"Kilsby? Police are hot on the trail." I laughed. "Trouble is, the trail stretches from here to town and back, and that's only the team working in Haxford. It doesn't count other people who might have followed him from other towns. According to these fairground people, he was a nasty piece of work." I munched on the sandwich and swallowed. "Did you have much to do with him?"

"No, not really. After he asked them, I dealt with the town hall mostly, and I met him there once. Then he came over and introduced himself yesterday. That's when he asked about private eyes. Oh, and he stopped by after you brought him back, but he didn't hang about. He had to go to Bolton or something. Obviously fancied himself, which is more than I did." She gave a naughty chuckle. "The beefcake he had with him when he was off to Bolton was quite tasty, though but."

Ossie. Again. "Spoken for," I told her. "Sorry, Sandra. You lose."

"Nothing new there then."

She perched on the upturned bread trays which had held her buns, and for a few minutes, we watched George Ibble further up the field, still trying to drill some sense of discipline into Banjo.

The dog's playful, if unwanted antics must have

sparked something in Sandra. "Do you remember the Wool Fair when you were a kid, Chrissy?"

I swallowed the last of my sandwich. "I've never forgotten it. Mam and Dad used to bring us here on the first weekend every year, and again on the bank holiday Monday, the last day before it shut down."

"Same for me. And it weren't just the fair, was it? I mean, when I were a kid, we'd come down to Barncroft's Meadow during the long summer holidays, picking blackberries or looking for fish in the river and frogs on the banks." She gave a fat chuckle "And the hours I spent here as a teenager with some lad… Oh dear, if my old dad had found out, he'd have leathered me." Her humour faded. "Our Ulrika didn't care what I knew when she was that age. She just told me to mind my own business. Is it me getting old, or what?"

I recalled that we had similar problems with our daughter, Ingrid, and by the time she was nineteen she had shipped out to the coast to try her luck as a pub/club singer. She was still there. No big star, but making a living. Sandra's words also reminded me of Gina Kilsby and her disinterested attitude to her father.

"It's a different world," I replied eventually. "They don't have the same inhibitions as we had. You don't have grandchildren yet, do you?"

"Perish the thought. You have the one, don't you?"

I nodded. "Bethany. Simon's little girl, and we're bringing her to the fair tomorrow. It helps recapture that innocence from all those years ago, but I don't imagine it'll be long before she's as independent and wilful as your Ulrika and our Ingrid." Before we could sink into total nostalgia, I said, "The fair must be different for you this time. Back then you were, sort of, partying, but now, you're working. It's always different on the other side of the counter."

"This is true. Even so, it's like some kind of other planet. Hell, I can't even understand the ruddy music anymore."

"And there, I'd have to agree with you." I drank the last of my tea and made a point of checking my watch. "Dennis is due here anytime, so I'd better get moving."

"And I'd better get on with the feeding the five thousand."

She disappeared and I sat watching George and Banjo for another couple of minutes before making my way from the back of the van to the front. Demonstrating my impeccable timing. I emerged in time to see Kilsby's pickup truck negotiating its way through the crowds, followed by the untidy and unwashed dark blue van belonging to Haxford Fixers.

I hurried across until I was alongside the pickup's route, and waved Dennis to a stop. He let the window down.

"Couldn't you have left it at the car park, Dennis?"

"I were gonna, but that plonker on the entrance wanted to charge me a fiver. I told him, I said, it belongs to the fairground, you banana. Why do you think the fair's name's written on the side? But he would insist. In the end I told him to get stuffed and he's gonna report me to the town hall. Says he knows where I live. Came on like something out of The Godfather. Berk."

"Right. So did Tony have to follow you all the way in?"

"Course he did. That barmpot were gonna charge Tony a tenner, never mind a fiver for parking the van. Anyway, forget him. Where do they want this thing?" He tapped the steering wheel indicating the 'thing'.

"I'll show you." I hurried round the vehicle, climbed into the passenger seat and pointed straight ahead. "Keep going past the dodgems, and then turn left towards the river." I waved my hand at the area closer to us. "And for pity's sake, watch these children."

"I'm watching 'em, I'm watching 'em."

It was difficult for him. Well, it would be, wouldn't it? When people are wandering around a funfair, the last thing they expect are a brace of commercial vehicles trying to get through. Eventually, we made the accommodation area and while he and Tony turned the firm's van round, ready for leaving, I took the keys from my husband, soothed Kaiser again, and knocked on Rachel's door.

Ossie greeted me with a broad smile. "Come in, Mrs Sherlock."

I frowned at his levity and followed him in. "My husband's here." I hoped the announcement would make him a little less frivolous, but it didn't. "He's brought Frank's pickup back and he wants paying."

He dug into his jeans and came out with a wad of

banknotes. Oh, God, I wished it was me digging into his jeans. I snapped my easily-led mind back to reality.

"You said a hundred, didn't you?" He peeled off five twenties and handed them to me.

"I'll get the invoice for you."

"Forget it. It won't go through the books. It's Frank's private transport, innit?"

"Was Frank's. He's dead."

"Whatever. You wanted a plan of the ghost train." He led the way to the table where a single sheet of A4 lay. "All there, the exhibits all marked out and the cross is where they found Frank. Near the Dracula puppet."

You have this impression of fairground folk as dirty, unwashed, but as I leaned over to look at the plan, I caught a nostril full of his aftershave and it almost made me giddy again. I controlled myself with the question of why he would use aftershave when he obviously hadn't shaved.

I picked up the sheet, backed off from the Hugo Boss or whatever he was wearing, and studied it. Studied the diagram, I mean, not his aftershave. As I anticipated, it was like a maze, but the track of the cars was clearly marked. "Just one thing. Could you mark out the rear access door?"

He moved to the sink and took out a pencil from the drawer – I daren't ask what a pencil was doing in the cutlery drawer – and drew a cross on one side of the outer wall. "There you go."

I folded the sheet neatly in half and tucked it in my bag. "Thank you. I'd better get on with earning my fees."

"And you'll keep us informed?"

"Naturally. Have the police had anything more to say to you?"

"Not yet, but we're expecting them."

"Just one question before I go. How many know about the access door at the back? I only found it by accident."

"Trying to narrow the field down, eh?" He laughed. "Everyone who works for Ketchak's Funfair knows about it. The ghost train might have been Frank's personal project, but we all know where we're up to if we need to get into it."

Not a very useful answer.

I came out of the caravan to find Tony Wharrier leaning on the firm's van, soaking up the afternoon sun, and no sign of my erstwhile.

"He's gone to look at the donkey driving the dodgems."

Dennis and Tony had been friends and workmates for much of their lives. As tall as my husband, Tony was slender, a little lugubrious but not as obsessed, slightly more erudite than Dennis in that he read magazines other than *Classic Motors*.

Even so, his explanation puzzled me. "The dodgems are driven by a donkey?"

"Donkey engine, Christine." As polite as ever, he never referred to me as Chrissy. "The generator's driven by a Gardner 150 engine, the kind they haven't used in lorries and buses since the sixties. And you know what Dennis is like with engines."

I sighed. "I'm really looking forward to getting old, you know. Maybe he'll think of me as a classic when I get there."

He smiled. "I'm sure he thinks the world of you."

"Probably. How are Valerie and the lads?"

"All fine, thanks. Craig's at long last decided to marry his girlfriend. Well, you know, they've been living together for about six years. September or October, I think. I'll make sure you and Dennis get an invite."

"Don't forget Lester."

His smile disappeared. He and Lester Grimes didn't get on. "He'll turn up for the party whether we invite him or not."

At that moment, Dennis came back, his eyes glazed in wonderment. "Gardner 150. What a piece of tackle. Takes me back some years, that. I'm telling you... oh. Hiya, Chrissy. Everything all right?"

I handed him the money and told him to forget about the invoice. "They're not bothered."

"Typical. I could have saved the ink and paper."

"And put the pennies towards the cost of a Gardner 150?" Before he could reply, I went on, "Don't you dare forget that we're taking Naomi and Bethany, er, here tomorrow for the fair."

"Aw. Do I have to? I mean work—"

"Can survive one Saturday without you, and I promised that child."

"So what's wrong with Simon?"

"I said I promised her, not Simon, and anyway, with a potential murder on his hands, he'll likely be working. I want you home by one o'clock tomorrow and don't be late."

"I'll make sure he's there, Christine," Tony assured me, and they climbed into their van.

With them gone, armed with my plan of the ghost train, I decided it was time I beat a retreat, too. Right now, I had no clue who to talk to or what to talk to them about, which is not a happy situation for a private eye. And besides, I had other calls to make, and first on the list was CutCost for our weekly shop.

Chapter Ten

CutCost was on Huddersfield Road, closer to the town centre than the Haxford Arms, and as the town's only major supermarket, it was so much busier, especially at half past two on a Friday afternoon.

Dennis would come with me now and again, usually once a month when we needed to restock the freezer, and he did nothing but complain. He always says it's because he doesn't like shopping and he doesn't like spending money, but I think it's because they don't sell engines. I always feel it necessary to point out that buying groceries is not 'shopping', not by my definition anyway, and if we didn't spend the money, he would starve to death. Come to that, with his appetite, he would be pleading malnutrition in a matter of hours.

Another thing we disagreed on was my habit of driving into a parking spot instead of reversing in. He says it's because I'm hopeless at reversing, but it's not true. I may not be the world's best but I can do it. However, neither of us is disabled and we don't have young children with us so we were not allowed to park in the reserved spots for such categories. We were part of the riff-raff, the hoi-polloi, and the spaces for the masses were a bit tight. If I reversed in, we would have a struggle getting the bags to the rear of the car. By driving in I could get the bags in the boot easier.

CutCost sold just about everything, including a range of electrical and electronic goods, clothing, mobile phones, clothing, small household appliances like kettles, microwave ovens, vacuum cleaners, clothing, music and videos, and did I mention clothing? They carried a range of low-cost fashion wear, shoes, undies, plenty of children's clothes, and footwear from trainers all the way up to quality (allegedly) leather shoes and matching handbags.

They also had a cafeteria, which was my first port of call for a pot of tea, in proper if cheap, china cups, and a scone with jam and cream. I wasn't too worried by the calorie intake. By the time I'd walked round the store, carried the groceries out and stowed them in the car, got them home and hauled them into the house, I'd burn off any excess. The calculations were based on my confident belief that a scone with jam and cream weighed in at about 100 calories and not the 600 and something Dennis claimed. I'd never actually checked it. I just knew he was wrong.

And while I sat there, relaxing, mentally preparing myself for the fight in the food hall, my favourite description of getting round the crowds in the shop, I studied the floor plan of the ghost train.

It was not my favourite type of fairground attraction. If I want a fright, I'll study the press speculation of forthcoming gas price increases. I never watched horror movies, and these days, I felt that the line between horror and science fiction had become blurred. Not that I watched sci-fi either. I remember ET, but I was a teenager at the time, so it didn't really do anything for me. My brother, Stephen, was into things like Star Wars and Star Trek whereas I just wanted to know how I could get a figure like Princess Leia.

Using the plan, I followed the anticlockwise track of the cars as they went through the ride, and tried to decipher the labels Ossie had added to it. DRC was fairly easy. Dracula. But it was the cross marking the location of Kilsby's body which made the acronym so simple to crack. Gina said he went in to attend to the Dracula puppet. Similarly, FKN wasn't difficult to translate as Frankenstein, and neither was ZMB (zombie) but I struggled with WFM, and for some time I wondered about GNT. Did it mean riders would be in need of a gin and tonic when they got that far, or was there some monstrous mythical creature waiting there? A quick call to Rachel soon put me right.

"WFM is Wolfman and GNT is the guillotine where some woman has had her head chopped off and the executioner holds it up."

I did notice that the Dracula puppet was at the back of the trail and comparatively close to the rear access. Only a matter of a few yards. So it would have been easy for the attacker to let himself in, shoot Kilsby and then get out. The car would do the rest. This did not tell me who, but it gave me an insight into the how.

Scone, jam, cream demolished, I ran a quick check on the full-length dresses for Jocelyn's wedding in the summer, decided I needed something a little more upmarket, and made my way down to the food hall where I began the weekly battle of the buying-in.

Despite the size of the store's windows, walking round CutCost meant interior lighting only; certainly for the first half of the journey which took me through fresh fruit and vegetables, dairy products like fresh milk, yoghurt, little dessert pots, then onto cheese and butter, fresh(ish) meat, pies, pizza, bacon, sausages, and the like, through long-life milk, canned fruit and other desserts, and finally to the bread aisles at the very bottom of the store. The layout had always irritated me. If someone called in for say, a loaf of bread, they had to walk all the way through the store to get it, which in turn meant the temptation for impulse buying was there. How could anyone walk past the confectionery without being tempted to buy a bag of liquorice allsorts?

After bread, by which time, the trolley was already half full, I had to cross the centre aisle, for alcohol, mixers and soft drinks, where a blaze of sunlight shone through the windows beyond the checkouts.

That's when it hit me.

If Kilsby was already in the ghost train when the attacker came through the rear access, the momentary daylight would have attracted his attention, he would have looked in that direction, and the shooter would have hit him in the forehead. Yet Simon told me he had been hit in the temple. He can't have been looking at the shooter, and putting all this together, it meant said shooter was in the ghost train when Kilsby went in.

It was this kind of logical deduction which separated us detectives from the mass of humanity who resented us, especially the crooked masses.

"We'd already worked that out, Mam," Simon told me when I rang him to report my assessment. "But who was it?"

"I don't know." Having already dropped biscuits, cereals and tinned peas, beans, carrots, and soup in the trolley, I was wandering along the freezer aisles and it was quite busy, which was fortunate. It helped me keep my irritated voice down. I threw in two bags of oven chips, the only food Dennis knew how to cook without setting fire to the kitchen, and said to Simon, "But when I find out, I'll let you know. And don't forget, we're taking Bethany and Naomi to the Wool Fair tomorrow."

"All arranged. Nam will be at yours for about half past one. Hey and don't spoil Bethany too much."

"Don't be silly. That's what grandchildren are for. Spoiling. And I do wish you'd call Naomi by her proper name."

"She prefers Nam, and doesn't Dad call you Chrissy?"

There was no mother-ish answer to that, so I rang off and made my way round to tissues, toilet rolls and kitchen towels. Once through there, I remembered Cappy the Cat's Dennis-esque appetite, and collected a dozen tins of his favourite food... well, I say it was his favourite, but it's not like I asked him. He got what he got and that was it.

He had no choice in the matter. From there, I made my way to the checkout anticipating a bill about the same as the monthly council tax charge, and joined a queue of three people.

In common with most supermarkets, acceding to the demands of irate parents and dentists, CutCost no longer displayed sweets at the checkouts. Instead, they displayed batteries of the kind both Dennis and I didn't pick up the previous day. I was tempted, but with a pack of four at just under four pounds, I thought better of it. Benny's Bargain Basement would sell me twenty for a pound and given the amount of use the remotes got, Dennis never stopped to count the number of times he had to replace them.

It was about quarter past four when I came out and loaded the car. If he were with me, Dennis would whine over the bill, and you might think he had a point considering we were only catering for him, me, and a moderately sized cat, but feeding Dennis was like shovelling food into a bottomless pit. There's an old joke about a dead rat and two stale loaves. Dennis would wolf down the bread while waiting for the rat to cook, and after that, he'd still come back for dessert and snacks.

It wasn't the best time of day for driving through any town, and Haxford was no exception. Friday afternoon, the world and Haxford was setting about the weekend, and much of the traffic was piling towards the Wool Fair, which happened to be in the same direction I was going, at least until I reached the fork for Derbyshire Road where the Wool Fair traffic shot off to the right, and where I carried on to join Moor Road and the climb up to Bracken Close.

And throughout the twenty-minute journey, I kept thinking about the death of Frank Kilsby. 'Who' Simon asked, and I still had no answer other than a cast of suspects which would be the envy of any James Bond movie. Just as important was the 'why'. Turning off the southern, town centre bypass for Moor Road, I qualified that question by asking myself 'why now?'

Kilsby himself admitted that there were plenty of people amongst his crew who didn't like him, but many of them had been with him for some time, so why wait until Haxford Wool Fair to get rid of him? It would have been better to kill him off in, say, Liverpool, Leeds, Manchester, or any other big city where crime was more prevalent than a poky little, former wool town nestling in the shadow of Huddersfield. Committing the crime here made it big news. I suppose it would have been front page stuff in Huddersfield or Barnsley, too, whereas in the big cities it might rate mention on the front page, but the detailed story would be relegated to an early inside page.

When I put the question to Cappy the Cat, he had no answers either. He simply snuggled up to me until I put down his food dish and small saucer of milk, whereupon he wolfed down the food, lapped up a little milk, took another slurp from his water, then made a bolt for the back door to check on the damage the airborne hooligans had done while he was confined to quarters. The last I saw of him, he was hopping over the fence into the Timmins's back garden, where he would no doubt leave his calling card for Fred and Barbara.

With the week's groceries put away, I settled down in the conservatory with a cup of tea, a couple of McVities digestives and my laptop.

Dennis sometime complained that I nagged him. Nonsense. All I did was prioritise those tasks which needed dealing with, and then made sure he did them. If he wanted nagging, he should have taken on the Kilsby killing. It wouldn't let me be in CutCost and it wasn't for letting go now.

Calling up my word processing software I began to ask the vital questions.

1. What was Kilsby doing in there? The Dracula puppet had fallen on someone.
2. Was that someone a member of the crew or a paying customer? A paying customer.
3. How could the puppet be made to fall? No answer.
4. Who would know so much about the construction of the exhibits to make the puppet fall? Everyone.
5. Would he have to be hidden in the background to ensure that the puppet fell on one of the cars? No answer.
6. Why Kilsby? Because Gina called him.
7. True, but why him in particular? Because he was the 'expert'.
8. Who alerted Gina? Someone coming off the ride, so she said.
9. Had the killer arranged for the puppet to fall? Considering he had to be in the ghost train before Kilsby, it was most likely.
10. How could he be sure Kilsby would

attend? He couldn't but it was a safe bet considering the victim's self-confessed 'expert' status.

Looking at the questions I focussed on those to which I had no answer, and all concerned the falling Dracula puppet.

As I read through it, I changed the answer to question 2 from 'a paying customer' to 'uncertain', but no matter which way I looked at the problem, it spelled out a deliberate act. But then, that was hardly a revelation. The use of the BB gun indicated a deliberate act, and whether it was designed to kill Kilsby (murder) or merely injure him (charge reduced wounding with a possible upgrade to manslaughter) would be one for the courts to decide.

That thought set my mind off on another track: the stolen rifle. According to Singer someone stole it, but Simon never got around to asking how that was possible. These stallholders were pretty keen when it came to keeping an eye on their equipment. He insisted someone had snipped the chain which anchored the gun to the stall. How was that possible? How long would his back have to be turned to give someone the time to steal the rifle, and how come he didn't notice it immediately?

I returned to my workstation in the front room, took out a notebook, went back to the conservatory and began to make a note of the questions I needed to ask and the people I had to ask them of. At the top of the list were Gina Kilsby and Jim Singer.

It was almost half past five when I ordered a whining Cappy the Cat back in. I left Dennis instructions to dig out and microwave a frozen shepherd's pie for his meal, and more importantly, exactly how long to leave it in the oven. The latter was vital, more so than telling him where to find it. Leave it to him, and he would micro-cremate it.

Happy that I was organised, I made my way out to the car. Sunset, according to my all-knowing smartphone, was sometime around half past eight and the fair would be open until eleven o'clock (possibly later on a Friday evening). Ample time to ask my questions and get home to feed the ever hungry cat because I knew Dennis wouldn't.

Chapter Eleven

Such was the queue of traffic that it was almost six when I pulled into the car park at Barncroft's Meadow and I was somewhat miffed at having to pay the £5 parking fee for the second time, despite showing the attendant – a different one this time – my ticket from earlier.

"You can't carry it over," he told me. "You park, you pay, if you leave and then come back, you pay again."

"But the sign says five pounds per day."

"Not interested." He held out his hand. "Fiver."

Recalling Dennis's comment earlier in the day, as I handed over the money, I asked, "Have you ever considered a career in organised crime? You'd be ideal for demanding protection money."

On any other assignment it wouldn't be a problem. I would bill the client for my expenses but in this case, the client was now in the mortuary, and I'd had a sizeable slice of his money before he departed this world. I couldn't really drop the expenses on his widow, could I? Or could I?

As I followed the increasing crowds into the fairground, I decided it would not be fair to Rachel (or Gina) to bill them for parking charges, but given their antipathy for me, and casually mentioning that

I was waiving them might just grant me the necessary goodwill, the leverage to get some answers out of them.

As I anticipated, the place was much busier than it had been earlier in the day and I saw a number of people that I knew, amongst them Barry Barnes with his wife, Vicky, and their two-year-old son, Brian, latest addition to the Barnes's male dynasty whose name began with the letter B. It was entirely in keeping with the family tradition. Forty years from now, I could see young Brian, currently relishing a ride on the teacups with his mother while his father videoed them on his phone, inheriting the family's High Street business, Benny's Bargain Basement.

The ghost train was still roped off as a crime scene, and I noticed young John Frogshaw and his best mate Owen (Digger) Trench arguing with a uniformed constable, presumably concerning the ride being closed. As I watched, they gave up the fruitless debate and shoulders hunched, tromped off towards the slingshot.

Radio Haxford's stand was up and running, and well-known local DJ Reggie Monk was introducing a four-piece rock band, The Sheepshanks. A mob of twenty-somethings they took the stage to a smattering of applause and began to make the most appalling racket with their guitars and drums, a noise so loud that it drowned out the young, female vocalist fronting them. I couldn't hear what she was singing, but I don't think it was 'In My Easter bonnet'. I also had to wonder if anyone had ever told them that a sheepshank was a knot, and nothing to do with the sheep which once flooded the moors, farms and, I suppose, the streets of Haxford. Then again, would they or anyone else care?

Rachel Kilsby had a long queue at her ticket booth and I wasn't prepared to wait. I tore a sheet from my notebook, wrote, *I need to talk to you urgently. Refuse and I'll get the police to take you in. Sandra's snack van ASAP*. I then walked to the front of the queue, excused myself and under a flood of murderous glances and accusations of queue-jumping, I slipped the note to her and walked away. I cast a quick glance over my shoulder and she was on her phone. A glower aimed at me told me she was taking me seriously. Many glowers from the queue told me I was not the most popular private investigator in Haxford at that moment.

Sandra had a long queue waiting for a feed but when she saw me, she backed off, left the counter to her sister and a moment later held up a large, white card upon which she'd written, BUNS STILL GOIN MISING. If I didn't know better, her spelling would have caused me to suspect her of sending the note to Kilsby, but I knew better. If Sandra Limpkin wanted to threaten anyone, she wouldn't waste ink and paper. She'd deliver the message verbally, face to face.

I acknowledged her with a nod and a shrug and instead of queueing up for a cup of tea I turned to look for Rachel.

I waited only about two minutes. First I saw Gina hurrying along past the waltzer in the general direction of the ticket booth, and not long after, Rachel was making her way towards me, her face set like thunder.

One thing you pick up in the police is assertiveness. They taught us how to control situations and how to maintain that control without resorting to the baton most of the time. If Rachel Kilsby thought she could intimidate me, she had another think coming. To quote my husband, I'd eaten bigger for breakfast.

"Who the bloody hell do you think you are?" Her opening salvo came in a voice which could probably be heard in Glossop, and before I could respond she went on to call me a series of names, most of which were unprintable, mainly because I wasn't sure how to spell them. I mean, what is a nosy ***************ious, jumped up* ******* *Yorkshire* ***** ******? The adjectives (and nouns) were interspersed with a level of effing and jeffing which would put to shame any alternative comedian determined to top the outrageous chart.

And try as I might, I couldn't get a word in to stem the tide of verbal abuse and aggravation. So much for assertiveness.

In the end she was shut up by the intervention of Barry Barnes, complaining about her language and his child's delicate ears. I thanked Barry who went back to his wife and son, queuing on the tail of Sandra's queue, while I finally got a word or two in.

"I understand how you feel, Rachel, but your late husband paid me a considerable amount of money to tell him who was threatening him. I was too slow, but I am determined to see the job through, and right now no one is talking to me, not even you, not even his daughter. I need you to stop evading the issues and start naming names." Before she could protest further, I pushed on. "Who could have arranged that Dracula puppet to fall?"

"How should I know?"

"You're doing it again. You should know. More than that, I think you do know, or you could at least narrow down the field."

The fury was still there in her voice. "Frank was the expert."

"I know, but Ossie told me there are any number of people who know the ins and outs of the ghost train operation. Now name them."

"Ossie's one of them. So is Willy Dodds, and Eddie Zannis. Gina knows some of it, and I do. But before you start accusing, I don't know how the puppets work and I wouldn't know how to make them fall. Right? Anyway, what does a falling puppet have to do with it?"

"It's what took Frank into the ghost train in the first place. And his killer was in there waiting for him."

"Garbage. Someone was watching for him going in, followed him and did the job."

"I already know that did not happen. Frank's murder was planned and the falling puppet was part of that plan. So who?"

"Talk to Ossie. He's manning the slingshot."

"I will. And I need to talk to Gina. Where will I find her?"

Some of Rachel's fire came back. "She had to relieve me on the ticket booth so I could come and speak to you."

"In that case, would you send her over to me,

please?"

"When I get back there, but don't expect anything more from her."

"We'll see about that. But you should know that I'm not going away. If I have to pester you people every day of the fair, I will."

If there was a hint of cold steel in her eye, it was complemented by the unmistakable threat in her voice. "That's the quickest way to get yourself hurt… or worse."

"I don't respond to threats."

"And we fairground folk don't make threats. We make promises."

She turned and walked away, stiff-backed, so confident that she had me worried. And she might have, but at that moment, Dennis rang.

"Where are you?"

"The Wool Fair."

"I thought that were tomorrow."

"It is. I'm working on a case, Dennis."

He clucked. "Poking your nose in again."

"I'm getting paid for it, so I have to poke my nose in. It's what I do. And why are you ringing? I left a note to tell you what to do about your tea."

"Yeah, but it didn't say why I have to do me own tea, did it? I meanersay, I've been doing proper work, not nattering to people about things that don't concern me."

I began to lose it. "You know when you service someone's car, Dennis, and it breaks down ten minutes after they collect it from you. Do you put right what you put wrong to make it break down?"

"Course I do."

"Well, this is the same thing. Frank Kilsby paid me to find out who threatened his life. They didn't just threaten his life, they took it, and I intend to find out who it was."

"Like I said, poking your nose in. It's a job for our Simon and his people."

"I'm helping them." I cut the call before he could raise any more objections.

There was no sign of Gina so I wandered away from the snack van, over to the dormant ghost train where I turned and looked back at Singer's shooting gallery. Essentially, it was a duck shoot. The ducks rolled past on a conveyor and the shooters had to try to knock them down with their pellets. I assumed that there would be some mechanism for righting them when they rolled out of sight and under the range before coming back. Higher up were proper targets, and as I watched, three people were at the range, and as they ran out of ammunition, Singer removed the paper targets and replaced them, then issued vouchers according to their score so they could collect prizes from the adjacent stand operated by a woman who was probably his wife. The smallest prize was a tiny, pram sized teddy bear, and to win it, they needed five vouchers. Looking at the number of vouchers he was giving out, I guessed they would need at least two or three attempts to win enough vouchers.

Several things occurred to me as I watched. Firstly, Singer was often in the line of fire, so he had to ensure no one was actually shooting when he walked across. Secondly and more important, while he was replacing the paper targets, his back was turned to the shooters, which meant anyone could have snipped off the rifle chain and then walked away with the weapon.

On the other hand, how many targets would he have been replacing early in the day when the fair wasn't so busy? Not many, so whoever the thief/ghost train shooter was, he must have moved quickly, and my earlier deductions also said, he must have been a member of the fairground crew.

It also dawned on me that it would be quite easy for a member of the crew to take the rifle. If a member of the public challenged him, he could always claim he was taking it for repair or something. Alternatively, if another member of the crew saw him, he could have been deep in the doggy-do. They would know that he was not authorised to do anything of the kind, and they would have brought the matter to the attention of the Rachel, Ossie, Gina, even the police after Kilsby's body was discovered.

It occurred to me that the same was true of anyone, not just a crew member, seeing someone wandering around with a rifle in his hand. The fair might not have been too busy, but there were too many people about for them not to notice and it would be almost impossible to hide the weapon.

A horrible notion occurred to me and the moment I thought of it, I knew it was true. Whoever shot Kilsby did not use one of Singer's rifles. Indeed, the difficulty of taking one of those weapons told me that it did not happen. It was a conspiracy, and Singer was part of it. He told Simon he'd had a rifle stolen knowing full well that when

Kilsby's body was discovered with a BB shot to the temple it would be assumed that his stolen rifle would be implicated as the weapon.

But why? Why would Singer choose to help someone dispose of Kilsby?

And then I remembered his words to Simon. 'Do you know how much it costs me to stand here? And now I'm not only a rifle down, but someone's actually nicked the thing.' He complained about losing money left, right and centre, and he was talking about the cost of replacing the rifle and the potential loss of custom because he had only five rifles not six. But what could he have been promised for aiding and abetting? Lower rent? A bigger percentage of the value of tickets he handed in at the end of the week? Or a cash sum?

The various scenarios developed quickly in my mind. 'Five hundred in cash, and all you have to do is lose one of your shooters and claim it was half-inched.' (Whenever I worked these things out, I always endowed the perpetrators with a poorer standard of spoken English than mine.)

There was, of course, another possibility: Coercion; intimidation. Singer had been threatened in order to ensure his cooperation. What was it Rachel said? Fairground folk did not make threats. They made promises. And wouldn't Singer know that? And wouldn't it be enough to make him toe the line, do as he was told.

That still did not tell me who, but it might help me narrow down the field. If it was someone promising lower rents or a greater cut from his ticket numbers, then it pointed the finger at someone near the top; Rachel or Gina or Ossie. With Frank gone, they would control the overall financial management of the fair. Unfortunately, in the more likely event that someone had paid Singer to mislead the police, it could be anyone. Indeed, in that case, it did not have to be a member of the crew. It could be an outsider, someone with a grudge against Kilsby, and it would be someone who had enough cash to buy a plan of the ghost train, and buy a means of disabling the Dracula puppet. Getting hold of a T-bar to let him in through the rear access wouldn't be a problem. They were fairly common. Dennis probably had one in his toolbox.

Then again, he would not need a plan of the ghost train. Hadn't Kilsby told me that the writer of the note could have been any one of a number of people he'd fired in the past? If that was so, then they would more than likely know how it was laid out.

Having reasoned all this out, what should I do? Common sense (and my husband) said I should take it to the police. Trouble was, at that stage Mandy would no longer be in charge of the case. Paddy Quinn would be top dog, and I knew Paddy. He would listen, tell me I was talking out of my bonnet, order me to mind my own business, then come to same conclusion but claim that he had thought of it independently.

Even if they decided to act, they would challenge Singer and all he had to do was brazen it out. Deny, deny, deny. Rachel, Gina, and Ossie had all hinted that these fairground folk were tough. Alongside some of them, Jim Singer didn't look it, but I remained convinced that he was every bit as cagey, cantankerous and bloody-minded as any other stallholder on the fair.

Would he get away with it if I challenged him? For a brief moment I considered trying my feminine wiles on him, but he was as old as me and judging by the familiarity between him and the woman dishing out the miniscule prizes, they were man and wife or man and significant other. Besides, unless I was working on a case of gathering divorce evidence, I tended to reserve my feminine wiles for Dennis, and only then when I wanted a new dress for a special occasion like Jocelyn's forthcoming wedding.

I decided to leave things as they were for the moment, and see what I could learn from Gina.

And talking of the daughter, there she was, face set grim, striding towards me.

Chapter Twelve

I suffered the inevitable tirade of verbal abuse before coming on strong with her the way I had with Rachel.

"You're not impressing anyone, young lady. I have a daughter about your age, and if she were here, she'd tear you to pieces for talking to me like that. You people think you're so tough? You haven't come across your average Haxforder yet. Now, I need answers and you are the start point because your father only went into that ghost train because you'd called him."

"I had to." Her voice was the defensive yelp of a puppy suffering a smack for misbehaving. "Someone said one of the puppets had fallen on him so I rang Dad."

"Why him in particular?"

"Because when it came to the ghost train, we always called Dad. I told you all this earlier."

"So you did. It doesn't mean I believe you and it doesn't mean the police will believe you either, so let's start narrowing down the field, shall we? Who reported the fallen puppet?"

Gina was getting really angry now. "How should I know? Just some punter. Do you know how busy we were this morning?"

"I do, but you weren't so busy that you hadn't the time to take some details off this person, were you? I know. I was at the shooting gallery behind you and while you did have a queue, it wasn't too big. Now who?"

"I told you, I don't know. He came round, got off the car, told me the puppet had fallen and went."

"And you let the ride go on. With a fallen puppet somewhere inside?" I cast my mind back to the emergence of the young woman and her two children and another angle occurred to me. "When that woman came out screaming that your father was dead, you weren't at the station. You came out a few moments later. You were already inside. So how did you know what had happened?"

"Are you accusing me—"

"I may very well be unless you can explain how you knew."

"I saw him on the screen."

"Screen? What screen?"

"You're some detective you are, aren't you? Did you not notice that the ghost train is double manned. Me and our Nick. I'm at the control station, he's at the cars getting the punters in and out."

In truth I hadn't noticed, but I buried that and listened to her.

"Nick's fifteen and he helps out on the ghost train. Just the simple stuff."

Another snippet of information which might or might not prove useful. "So you were at the control station and it has some kind of access screen showing you what's going on inside."

"It's like closed circuit telly and it's a laptop. It

lets us keep an eye out for problems. I saw the car stop, I saw the body under the car. I stopped the chain that tows the cars round, and went in. I told the woman the way out while I checked on it, and it was Dad. Right? The cops know all this."

"And they have the CCTV footage?"

"Yes. Is that it? Have you done shoving you oar in?"

"I need as much information as you can give me, so you'll have to do better than that, Gina."

"No. I don't have to do anything. You can go—"

"Don't say it. I had enough abuse off our stepmother earlier."

So she didn't say it. She just turned and stomped away.

I was shaking. Even during my years as a police officer, I couldn't recall coming on that strong with a suspect. It was so unlike me. Under normal circumstances I was Mrs-easy-to-get-on-with, cheerful, contingent, willing to argue my case, but not to the point of all-out war... except with Dennis. And yet, here I was browbeating this young woman, refusing to accept evasions, demanding the truth or else. It was unnerving, but the same time, it felt quite intoxicating, a power kick; I'm Mrs-don't-mess-with-me-or-you'll-be-sorry.

Coming down from the high, I decided I did not believe one word Gina had said. I could believe Rachel – just about – but not her stepdaughter. According to my theory, if that puppet really did fall on a paying customer he would have kicked up a bigger fuss than Gina pretended, and she would have almost certainly remembered him. Not only that, Gina would have seen it on the CCTV screen, and as far as I was concerned, the puppet and the customer and possibly even Gina, were all part of the plan to get Frank Kilsby into the ghost train.

"You know, you've got an awful lot of bottle for a little woman."

The voice stirred me from my self-congratulatory reverie. It was Ossie, standing alongside me, towering over me, turning my knees to jelly. Well, not exactly jelly, but producing slight tremors in tune with long held and almost dormant memories.

"You were watching?"

"And listening while I waited." He nodded to the long queue at Sandra's van. "You got answers out of Rache, you got answers out of Gina. They won't like that."

"I'm doing the job Frank paid me to do, the job you said I should carry on with."

"I did, but not to the extent of getting your head caved in. Make no mistake about it, Mrs Sherlock, those are two tough ladies. It goes with the kind of life they've led."

We began to walk together in the general direction of the ghost train and as we strolled along, my five foot four inch frame looking ridiculous alongside his six feet six, he expanded on his initial announcement.

"Take Gina, for instance. Pregnant at fourteen, lumbered with a son when she was just turned fifteen. Obviously, young Nick wasn't planned, but he was there and she had to grow up real quick. And because we're travellers, she had to educate the kid as well as bringing him up as well as doing her bit on the fair."

"Perhaps her parents should have kept a closer eye on her," I ventured.

He chuckled. "The process by which Nick was produced wasn't planned either. A drunken encounter behind the vans in a field outside Macclesfield. At least, that's the way she tells it."

My suspicion-ometer hit a peak. "You're the boy's father?" I put it as a question but I feared it sounded more like an accusation.

"Sorry. Wrong track. I'd have been twenty-five, twenty-six at the time, and I wasn't working the fairs. I didn't even know the Kilsby family existed. I was barely out of college."

The suspicion-ometer sank without trace, and the surprise-ometer leapt up to full scale. "You went to college?" I realised the level of astonishment in my tones, and the way he might interpret it: insulting. "I'm sorry. I didn't mean it to come out like that."

"That's okay. Most people can't believe it when they first hear it, but yes, I did several years of training in mechanical and electrical engineering. At the time, Frank was looking for someone to head up the technical side of the fair. You know. Setting up the rides, making sure they were safe, maintaining the gear. He took me on, but he didn't pay great. I made extra by helping out on the fair when it was running. Now, fifteen years later, I'm effectively his second in command… well, first in command now, I suppose, although ownership passes to Gina and Rache. They need me more than they ever did, which may be good from my point of view, but only if the fair survives."

I took that as a hint to something Rachel had told me on my second visit the previous day. "The loans?"

"Theoretically crippling," Ossie agreed. "The insurance should pay most of them off, but I haven't studied the policies yet, so I don't know if they cover murder. They were personal to Frank, not the company." He sighed. "I'll tell you something, Christine, in some ways Frank was a genius. Selling, for instance. He'd sell you a fur coat for use on the beach in Barbados, and you'd be happy to buy it. When it came to persuading the bank to lend him stupid sums of money, he sold them the dream and they were happy to give him the cash. A sales genius. But in other ways, he was an idiot. He's registered as the sole proprietor and for a one man band, albeit a large one man band, he was too ambitious. Take the slingshot as an example. Second hand, forty grand, he actually borrowed over fifty, and is it paying its way? Not a chance. Not yet. And the maintenance bills on it are horrendous. Didn't we have to go for fresh ropes yesterday?"

"And now that he's dead?"

"The bank will want their money. If the insurance won't cover it, they'll go for his estate, and the fair is his estate. If it all goes wrong, Gina and Rache could find themselves with nothing left but the dodgems and the waltzer, two rides which are forever breaking down. Worse than that, they could literally end up with nothing but the caravans."

That did not fill me with confidence, and once again I was concerned about the cheque I had paid into my account. I didn't want it returned 'refer to drawer', or whatever they wrote on bounced cheques these days.

He shook his head. "I told you, they're two tough ladies and they'll need to be even tougher to get through this."

"Well, I'm sorry, but we still need to know what happened to Frank, who carried out the attack, and before you say anything both I and the police are certain it was a targeted attack."

"And I bow to your superior knowledge, but be careful is all I'm saying." He waved around us. "Fairground folk. We keep ourselves to ourselves. Townies don't trust us. And we don't trust them. If you stumble across anything and you need help, don't keep it to yourself and don't rely on the filth. Come to me instead."

My hero!

As we made our slow way towards the ticket booth, I was a seventeen-year-old girl again and hopelessly in love with Simon Le Bon. This was getting ridiculous. There was work to be done and I really had to pull myself together.

I decided on a distraction. "Nick; Gina's son. How does he go on for schooling and stuff? I mean you're always on the move."

"Home schooling. He can read, he can write, he can add up. If he follows the Kilsby tradition, he'll never be anything other than a fairground hand, but I know Gina is trying to arrange something for him to sit GCSEs next year." Ossie laughed again. "Not that he has much chance of getting pass grades, and not that he's ever likely to need them who needs to study Dickens or Hardy to operate a ghost train? Everywhere we stand, some geek from the Education Department comes round and pokes his or her nose in. It's about the only time Gina keeps her mouth shut. She lets Nick talk for himself. And he's happy, you know. Maybe he should have mates his own age, but he gets on well with most of the permanent crew."

"Did Gina ever say who the father was?"

Ossie laughed again. "Someone named mind your own business. That's all Frank and Rache ever got out of her." He glanced at his watch. "Time I was getting someone to relieve Rache on the ticket booth."

When he checked the time, I automatically glanced over the West, where the sky was turning a glorious scarlet as the sun made its way to the horizon. A glance at my timepiece said it was half past seven. Doesn't time fly when you're enjoying yourself?

Ever eager to remain in his company, I said, "Just one last thing, Ossie. The Dracula puppet that allegedly fell on a passenger. The one Frank went in to repair. How are the animatronic movements controlled?"

"Animatronics?" There was that easy-going laugh again. "Where did you hear that word? Frank, I'll bet. They're nothing of the kind. That particular doll really is a puppet. It's suspended on thin wire and as the car passes, it trips a switch. The puppet comes down like Dracula flying in to bite your neck, but it stops a good couple of feet short of the punters' heads. The car then passes over a second switch, and that pulls the puppet back up to wait for the next car. If it really did fall and hit this whiner, other than him just getting the willies, then it means one of the wires must have worked loose."

"Difficult to arrange?"

"Not especially, but I don't understand… ah. I see what you're getting at? You think someone rigged it so that Frank would have to go in. Who? When? The train had been running for a couple of hours and no one else complained. So it had to have been done as that moaner was passing, or just before. No, sorry, girl, but I don't buy it. Whoever topped Frank was an opportunist. He got wind of Frank going into the ghost train, followed him and did the business. I'm sorry, Christine, but I have to go. You need to know anything else, shout me, but make it tomorrow, eh?"

"I'll do that."

I think there was a dreamy look on my face as he walked away. If only I were fifteen years younger… and didn't have a husband and family. A quick glance at my watch and the unlikelihood of getting any further forward on this fine evening confirmed that it was time to get myself home where I could daydream to my heart's content, and as I made my way to the car, I wondered if Dennis might be feeling up to a spot of exercise later.

Chapter Thirteen

He wasn't. And to be honest, by the time I got home, I was so tired that I was no longer troubled by the inner stirrings.

After I left Barncroft's Meadow I remembered I still hadn't bought batteries. No point whipping into town. Benny's Bargain Basement and the market hall, the best places for saving money, were both shut, so I called at the local Breakfast to Bedtime store on Moor Road. Their shops were owned by one of the supermarket giants, and the prices were marginally higher than you'd expect in say, CutCost, but it was handy, and at that hour, handy was good enough for me.

Only one of the two checkouts was in operation, and there was a fair queue, most of them buying in their Friday night beer, brandy, and Benson & Hedges. Dennis and I both liked the odd drink, but I usually bought the bottles and cans at CutCost. Neither of us were smokers. I tried it when I was about fifteen and didn't like it so I never touched tobacco again. Dennis had never smoked, and he was one of those men who actively went to town on people who smoked near him. That included Lester Grimes, the only one of the three Haxford Fixers to indulge. A partner in the business he might be, but he had to go outside for a smoke. It caused some argument, especially when it was raining, but Dennis refused to discuss it. "You can't smoke in the Sump Hole, but it doesn't stop you going there. You don't smoke in this workshop." It seemed odd to me that none of them appeared to realise smoking in the workplace was illegal, and when I mentioned it, Dennis wasn't interested. "I'm the senior partner, so my word is law in that workshop."

While I waited in the queue in Breakfast to Bedtime, I remembered I had a couple of scratchcards to cash in. Only about ten pounds but better in my purse than the lottery's bank. And we were taking Bethany to the fair on Saturday, so I needed to pay my lottery numbers on while I could.

There was man behind me carrying two four packs of Haxford Best Bitter and half a bottle of scotch in his basket. As the queue shuffled forward he became more and more impatient. It seemed to me that he was in hurry to get home and indulge in his alco-fest. It didn't help when the old man in front of me couldn't fathom out his chip and pin card. After three attempts he realised he was trying to pay with his fashion outlet loyalty card. Putting aside the question of why a man of his age would need a fashion outlet loyalty card, the checkout operator pointed out the problem and there was another delay while the customer dipped into his wallet and came out with his bank card. That didn't work either, probably because it was so mucked up, so in the end, he had to put in his PIN, but his eyesight wasn't the best, and he had to lean close to the reader to see the numbers.

I thought he'd get a round of applause when he finally picked up the loaf of bread and carton of milk that he'd bought, but he wasn't finished. He handed his lottery fast pay cards, and then took out a fiver to pay his numbers on.

"It's the wife" he explained. "She pockets the winnings so I'm hanged if I'll pay for them."

By now, two four packs and whisky was almost apoplectic and it didn't help when I handed over a pack of batteries and a packet of extra strong mints and my lottery fast pay ticket. It aggravated him even further when I paid for them with my debit card, and then gave the operator my scratchcards. "I want the cash back," I told the operator who had that look on her face which asked why I hadn't taken the ten-pound winnings off my bill.

"Thank God for that," I heard four packs and whisky mutter as I collected my winnings and went on my way.

He really needed to chill out, but I did notice that he wasn't using a card. He had cash ready in his hand. He was out of the shop and striding for home before I settled into my car.

I parked in front of Dennis's car. He would be out before me in the morning, but after such a trying day, he could come out and swap them over.

"I'll deal with it," he said when I told him, but he barely took his eyes off a repeat of *Top Gear* when he said it, which meant he would forget and then grumble about it on Saturday morning.

I tossed the new batteries on the occasional table in front of him, then made my way into the kitchen.

I'll say this for my old man. When he had to deal

with his own tea, he didn't leave a mess. He hadn't even bothered with a plate, but thawed and cooked the shepherds pie and eaten it straight off the plastic tray. The only thing left behind was an empty cup and the fork he'd used. I often considered keeping a supply of plastic forks in the house so he could use them for such emergencies (his description of having to cook his own tea) and leave absolutely nothing to be washed up.

What he didn't do – and I knew he wouldn't – was feed Cappy the Cat. Our precious moggie was almost as skilled as Dennis at putting on the injured act. He staggered into the kitchen in a passable impression of starvation and wrapped himself round my legs a couple of times until I put a dish down, whereupon, he devoured it in a matter of seconds and wandered off back into the front room and settled into a corner of the settee, ignoring both me, my husband, and the repeat of *Top Gear*.

I dug out a frozen jacket potato, thawed and cooked it, but unlike Dennis, I put it on a plate and stayed in the kitchen to eat. When I was through, I left the plate in the washing-up bowl (I wouldn't put the dishwasher on for such a tiny amount) made two beakers of tea and carried them through to the front room.

"Done poking your nose it, have you?" Dennis asked as Top Gear finished.

"Nothing like."

"Aye, well, Sandra's been on the phone asking about her buns, and our Simon said he needs a word. He's coming round at nine o'clock."

"Buns to Sandra, and what does Simon want?

Bethany's not poorly is she?" I knew right away that she couldn't be. If it was something like that, Simon wouldn't pay us a visit. He'd say so over the phone.

"He didn't say. Probably summat to do with work, which means he'll want to know what you know about Killjoy's murder."

I suppressed a yawn. With a visit to the fair tomorrow I decided I needed to go to bed early. "Yes, well, as I said, I'm not much further forward."

"How come? You were there most of yesterday and you've been there practically all day today."

"All day aside from the two hours I spent wandering round CutCost, bringing the shopping home, putting it away, feeding the cat and all the other stuff you never get around to doing."

"Aye, well, I have a proper job of work, don't I?" In an effort to avoid argument, Dennis pressed further. "So come on then. Tell me what you've found out."

I recognised the ploy for what it was. We didn't argue much. No more than any other couple who had been together for thirty years or more, and most of our spats were domestic; like going to the supermarket, like putting the groceries away, like feeding the cat. Dennis wasn't the most sensitive of men, but in this situation he could sense a major argument brewing, and one sure way to head it off was to ask about my day.

So I told him everything from my early visit and non-event chats with Rachel, Gina, Ossie, Sandra's complaints over her stolen buns, George Ibble and

Banjo, and the startling deductions which had occurred to me on my way round CutCost, and I concluded with the way Ossie disagreed with me.

"The trouble is, Dennis, I don't see how this can have been an opportunist crime. Kilsby was in the ghost train seeing to this puppet, and at that point the cars were still moving. So if someone sneaked in through that rear door, the passengers in those cars will have seen daylight, and so would Kilsby. Whoever shot him had to be in there before Kilsby went in. He was hiding somewhere."

Dennis took a few moments to think about the matter and then surprised me. "He was still in there afterwards, as well. He must have been."

"How come?"

"According to the way you're telling it, Kilsby was shot and fell on the tracks. The car hit him, and the woman and her brats legged it out of there, and Kilsby's daughter went in. Am I right sort of?"

"Yes. Almost. Gina Kilsby was on her way in before the woman came out. She'd seen what happened on the computer screen."

"Whatever. It's pitch dark in there and the cars had all been stopped. After she came out, our Simon went in, and it was only after that when the other people came out, those who were still in the cars. So, at no time was that ghost train completely empty. There was someone in them tunnels all the time. At least until our Simon and the other punters came walking out. Are you with me so far?"

I had the vaguest inkling of where Dennis was going with this. "Go on."

"If your shooter got out of the ghost train

through that back door, all those people in there would have seen daylight. Stands to reason, dunnit?"

He was right and I was annoyed because I hadn't seen it earlier. Who was the detective in our house? Me. Why, then, did I have to rely on an automobile obsessed husband to point out the obvious?

Dennis was not through. "I don't know who your shooter is, but he was still in there when our Simon went in."

At least I could disagree with him this time. "Not necessarily."

"Chrissy, it's—"

I held up a hand for silence. "Hear me out, Dennis. Simon went in through the exit door, where the cars come out. Those other punters you're on about came out on foot from the entrance, the door where the cars go in. After dealing with Kilsby, the shooter could have moved further along the train, waited for it to come to a stop, and when those other customers came out, he could have mingled with them."

Dennis screwed up his face. It was the same gesture he used when looking at a car and preparing to tell the owner just how much it was going to cost. "He'd be taking a big risk, and if it was someone they all know and that Gina spotted him, he'd have been knee deep in sump oil."

"He'd already taken a risk going in there and shooting Kilsby. He didn't have much to lose, did he? You're half right. He could have hidden until Simon and the other customers came out, but equally he could have mingled with them, even if he'd had to wait until they came out."

We left it at that. Dennis went back to another repeat episode of *Top Gear*, and I sat twiddling my metaphorical thumbs until Simon arrived at about half past nine. After a brief chat with his father, he and I moved to the kitchen where I made fresh tea, and we sat at the table.

"Everything's all right with Naomi and Bethany?"

"Couldn't be better," he agreed. "We'll have trouble getting Beth to sleep tonight. She's too excited about tomorrow."

"So what was it you wanted, Simon?"

"It's not good news, Mam. Paddy Quinn's on the warpath over this business at the Wool Fair. He's told me to find out everything you know, and then tell you to keep away from it."

I could feel my anger building. "And he didn't have the guts to tell me himself? I hope you told him where to get off."

My son held his hands up in surrender. "I can't do that, Mam. Remember, I'm an *Acting* DC. If I step out of line, he can kick me back to uniform. Once my promotion is secured, then I can argue the toss with him."

"Very well, we'll try another approach. You tell Paddy Quinn that I want to speak to him personally, and I'll read him the riot act. He might have some control over you, but I am a free agent, a private citizen and he can't stop me doing whatever my clients ask as long as it's not illegal, and it isn't illegal."

Simon smiled. "I had an idea that would be your

reaction. I'll tell him, and he'll likely catch up with you sometime tomorrow."

"Good. I'll look forward to it, but tell Naomi she might have to look after Bethany while I bite Paddy's head off. Now, why you're here, tell me where you people are up to. Did you find the BB gun yet?"

"No. Mandy ordered a couple of uniforms to put their wellies on and get in the river, but it hasn't turned up yet."

"Right, well, let me tell you what I've learned today."

From there, I detailed my conversations with Rachel, Gina, and particularly Ossie and his opinions on the state of Ketchak Fair's finances. Once he'd made a few notes, I told him of the brief debate his father and I had just before he arrived.

He did not take the news well. "I'm going to look a right banana when this gets out, aren't I? This killer was still in there when I went in to check on Kilsby."

"I'm sure he was, Simon, but remember, he kept himself hidden from Kilsby, so hiding from you would be child's play."

"You were there, Mam. You didn't notice anything when those other punters came walking out of the ghost train?"

"No. But why would I? For all I know, one of the fairground crew could have been amongst them. I only know a few of them."

Simon put his notebook away. "All right. I'll pass all this to Mandy and get her to let Paddy know what you said. And I'll likely see you sometime

tomorrow, but I'll probably be working."
"At the Wool Fair?"
"Odds on," he agreed.

Chapter Fourteen

Another glorious morning greeted Cappy the Cat and me at a quarter to eight on Saturday. I'd planned to lie in until about half past nine but much slamming of car doors and unnecessary revving of engines confirmed that Dennis had not registered my words when I told him I'd blocked his car in the previous night. I know he said, "I'll deal with it," but that was a stock response. If I said to him, "I've packed my cases and I'm leaving you to live as a hermit on the Isle of Lundy," he would reply, "I'll get it sorted." He once tried to claim it was because he was getting hard of hearing, but that was not the case at all. When he was concentrating on TV programmes concerning cars and/or engines, even repeats, it wouldn't matter what I said, he would promise to either sort it out, deal with it, see to it, or some such similar phrase.

I was not best pleased to be woken an hour and a half before I'd planned, but I got up anyway, shooed Cappy the Cat from the bed and the room, and made my way to the bathroom. I would speak to Dennis when I'd showered and had breakfast.

Twenty minutes later, dressed for the day, kettle on the boil, a bowl of muesli awaiting my attention, I let Cappy the Cat out through the conservatory door and while he terrorised the local birdlife, and paid his morning call on the Timmins's lawn, I set a dish down for him, and finally carried my breakfast through to the conservatory.

This was my quiet time, my thinking time, that time of day when I planned ahead. I had to speak to Paddy Quinn. Well, I didn't have to but I would because I objected to the way he tried to use my son to get me out of the way. That would need to be dealt with early because top priority was a three-year-old child overwhelmed with excitement at the prospect of a visit to the fair. Somewhere along the line I would have to give a little thought and attention to my two cases; the murder of Frank Kilsby and Sandra Limpkin' stolen buns… although, short of actually catching the thief red handed, I did know what I could do about the latter.

As for the former, I needed to speak to Jim Singer. I remained convinced that he knew more than he was letting on. Well, he hadn't let anything on because no one had spoken to him.

All this would need some delicate manoeuvring because entertaining Bethany was top of the list. She was my first grandchild, only grandchild to date, and I shamelessly doted on her.

Cappy the Cat returned looking pleased with himself. He had obviously seen off the local chapter of the garden bird hell's angels, and presumably left his calling card in Fred Timmins's garden. He sidled up to me asking for a bit of attention, but it didn't last long. He either saw or smelled his dish, and disappeared into the kitchen to see what goodies awaited him.

People sometimes asked why we named him Cappy the Cat when it was so obvious that he was a cat. The answer lay in our surname and Dennis's nickname. He had always been known as Cappy. When we decided to name the cat after him – they were both obsessed, Dennis with engines and food, Cappy the Cat with his territory and food, both lazy, both moody when they chose – it was natural to add 'the cat' to Cappy the Cat's name to avoid confusion. It would sound odd calling Dennis for a visit to the vet for worming.

Breakfast over, interim plans for the day in hand, I rang Dennis to remind him that we were taking Bethany to the fair.

"Do you know how much work we've got on?"

"No, and I don't care. That child is looking forward to grandma and granddad taking her to the fair, and I'm not having you skiving off this afternoon."

"I'm not skiving off. It's just that—"

"You've had a shedload of work come in and you can't make it. I've heard it all before. I want you back here and ready to pick up Naomi and Bethany by two clock, so you'd better be here for one so you can shower and shave."

"Shower and shave? For visiting the Wool Fair?"

"You heard me."

"I had a shower last night."

"Well, you can have another today. It's not illegal, you know, and you don't have to worry. You'll only scrub the grease away, not your skin. You'll not disappear like a Cheshire cat."

That, I decided, would teach him to wake me

ninety minutes early on a Saturday morning.

Settling in the conservatory again, I thought about the inquiry so far. Frank Kilsby had paid me £400 and I was making less progress than Cappy the Cat when he was chasing off the birds. At least they did fly off for a while even if they did come back. I had no firm suspect and only a lot of tittle-tattle.

So what did I need?

A camera? I couldn't see what use it would be but considering we were taking Bethany to the fair, it might be worthwhile carrying it. Mine was a Sony a7 II Mirrorless model. I don't know what mirrorless means. I'd never considered it any use for applying eye shadow, lipstick and so on. It came in at just shy of £1200 and Dennis almost had a heart attack.

"I need it for my business," I told him.

"I need spanners for my business, but I can buy a shop full for that price."

"My camera won't break when I press the button too hard," I retorted, a reference to his habit of breaking those spanners when called upon to loosen anything tougher than bicycle wheel nuts. It was down to his habit of buying the cheapest wrenches he could find, and by cheap I mean rock bottom junk. I've seen him work with packaged sets of ten keys from shops like Benny's Bargain Basement, which were so inferior that no self-respecting, vintage Meccano junkie would trust them.

But even allowing for Bethany, did I need to carry a fortune in camera to the Wool Fair? I did not. My smartphone had an adequate camera app and it would do nicely. And in the event that I took pictures which might be relevant to Frank Kilsby's death, it would also avoid raising suspicion, although why my all-singing, all-dancing Sony should arouse suspicion I don't know. It was probably me being suspicious of peoples' tendency to being suspicious of people who did not fit the Haxford template, and fancy cameras were not the norm for Haxford... unless you were a reporter, or a cop, or a private eye, or anyone else who might need to carry a large camera.

A notebook and pen were essential for any PI. And I hadn't made enough use of mine. As a police officer I soon learned never to trust anything to memory, and yet that's exactly what I had been doing for most of the last two days. But did I want to lug a springbound notebook around when I was supposed to be entertaining Bethany? Fortunately, I had the perfect thing in my bag. Dennis bought me a smashing pocket diary with its own pen for Christmas. All pink and glitter. So was the pen. I say Dennis bought it. I actually bought it and wrapped it and applied the gift tag. He just scribbled 'Harry Xams' on the gift tag and signed it. At least, it looked like 'Harry', but I think it was supposed to be 'Happy'. I couldn't complain. I mean, I could, but he'd made worse errors during our thirty odd years together. Witness the time he almost forgot my birthday, and went haring round to the paper shop before leaving for work. He came back with a card that read, *congratulations on passing your driving test*. I was a bit annoyed. I was a qualified police driver years before I met him.

Having prepared everything I was likely to need and got myself dressed up for the afternoon in my Blondie tee and comfy jeans, it was only eleven o'clock and I had nothing left to do until Dennis came home and got himself ready, or until Naomi and Bethany turned up, so I returned to the kitchen for a necessary cup of tea, and then to the conservatory only to find a pigeon pecking away at Cappy the Cat's food bowl. I chased it out, and mentally cursed that idiot cat. I had no idea where he was but I'd lay odds on the Timmins's garden again. We reckoned he didn't like Fred and Barbara Timmins, which is why he spent so much time over there, making a mess of their lawn, their flower beds rather than ours. How did it go, that old adage of 'not on your own doorstep'?

And now I was ready and I had a couple of hours to kill before Dennis would show his face, and it would be half past one before Naomi and Bethany turned up. Nothing to do but while away the time. I suppose I could have planned my next vlog, but the moment I considered it, the rebellious thought hit me: *on a Saturday? Get a life, woman.*

Well, I had a life and very relaxed and easy going it was, too, but what do you do when you hit this kind of impasse? Hoover the carpet, dust the furniture that needed dusting, or laze about the conservatory and look forward to Cambridge in the summer and my niece's wedding.

Cappy the Cat reappeared, made his presence known by rubbing up against my leg, then sniffed at his food bowl before turning round and looking for the offending pigeon which had left its scent there.

The sun shone through the windows, increasing the room temperature, and on the window sill the little pendulum of our decorative carriage clock swung backwards and forwards, backwards and forward, with hypnotic regularity, and I felt my eyelids getting heavy…

I woke with a start. I'd been dreaming. An evil clown reaching under the big top tent, stealing a tray of buns, taunting me with them, waving the tray before me then pouring all twelve into his mouth in one foul moment of gloat and gluttony.

"Stolen buns on the brain," I muttered as I glanced at the clock which had put me to sleep.

WHAT? Five minutes to one? How was that possible?

Dennis would be home soon, daughter-in-law and granddaughter wouldn't be far behind him. We'd be on our way to the Wool Fair in less than an hour.

The side door rattled, a key turned, and Dennis walked in. Perfect timing.

I moved to the kitchen as he came in "Did someone burn the mill down?"

"Yes, very funny."

"You're early," I pointed out. "Remind me to take an umbrella this afternoon because you're never early which means it's sure to rain."

"Shurrup, will you? Geronimo has to take his missus to the fair, and Grimy knocked off early so he could sink a few in the Sump Hole."

"I'll make some tea. Get your shower and change. Naomi and Bethany will be here soon."

"Any danger of a butty to go with that? The

Snacky's rubbish when Sandra's not there."

"Will you tell Sandra that when we get to the fair? Just get on with it, Dennis. I'll make you something."

He took the hint and disappeared. I cut him a cheese doorstep and made fresh tea. There was no danger of it cooling off. I knew Dennis too well. A five minute shower for him was about forty seconds. He was in and out so fast he hardly had time to get wet.

And as I went through these routine actions, I realised that I was seriously wound up. Nodding off to sleep like that, Dennis turning up earlier than expected, it got me all flustered, threw out my planned, leisurely schedule. I took a few deep breaths. Why so worked up? We were only spending an afternoon at the fair.

The moment I finished getting his sandwich ready, the side door opened again and a little pink blur hurtled in, shouting, "Nanna, Nanna," and as I turned from the worktop, Bethany threw herself into my arms.

She was followed at a more sedate pace by her mother, Naomi, who greeted me with a cheerful smile. "Afternoon, Chrissy. Having a good one?"

"Not so you'd notice."

This young woman, married to my son Simon for the last four years, was the daughter I wanted but never really had. We saw Ingrid twice a year if we were lucky, but I saw Naomi most days. She and Simon only lived a few streets away, and we'd already agreed that when Naomi went back to work, as soon as Bethany started school, I would collect our granddaughter every day and look after her until either Naomi or Simon got home. Odds on it would be Naomi. Simon would be far too busy establishing himself as a detective.

And talk of the devil, as Naomi insisted I sit and entertain Bethany while she made tea, Simon walked in. They made a handsome couple, Simon standing about six feet, good looking, rugged and muscular, Naomi a curvy, striking beauty, with diamond blue eyes and the most enviable stream of dark hair cascading over her shoulders. She was not a native Haxforder. They met at Leeds University, but for all that she came originally from somewhere outside Manchester, she had settled well in our little town, and became a native by marriage.

"I thought you were working?" I said.

"I am, but I'm not meeting Mandy until this afternoon. Did you phone Quinn?"

"I don't beat Paddy Quinn up over the phone, luv. I'd rather do it in person."

We settled in the conservatory where Bethany proceeded to tease Cappy the Cat. He tolerated it so long before scowling and walking away from her, making for the front room and his basket.

Then Dennis arrived. "Hey up, Simon, Naomi. Day off, is it, lad, or are you just skiving?"

"You should know better, Dad. I'm a copper. Never off duty."

Munching on his sandwich, he ran an appreciative eye over Naomi's denims and tight t-shirt. "You're looking good, lass."

This came as a shock to me. Dennis complimenting some woman – albeit his daughter-in-law – on her appearance?

"I was looking at a couple of e-type Jaguars in a magazine the other day, and you remind me of the way the bodywork curves.

That was more like the Dennis I knew so well. "Don't be offended, Naomi," I advised her. "Almost everything and everyone reminds him of cars."

Naomi laughed. She really was a most pleasant young woman. "What does Chrissy remind you of, Dennis?"

"A well-tuned Morris Minor 1,000 in mint condition." There was a smug look on Dennis's face which told me he thought he'd just complimented me.

I ignored the advice I'd given Naomi. "That's the little fat one, isn't it?"

"Well, I wouldn't say fat. Just nice and round."

My son and his wife laughed. I didn't.

"You're digging your own grave, Dad," Simon said, and stood up. "If we're all ready, shall we get going? Beth's dying to go on the roundabouts."

"You christened her Bethany," I said and finished my tea.

Chapter Fifteen

"A flaming fiver?" Dennis had one of his apoplectic fits of outrage when he saw the sign as we tagged onto the end of the queue shuffling its slow way into the car parks.

"And you can't claim you're one of them today, can you?" I pointed out. "Not when you're in your own car."

"Yeah, but five quid to leave the car on a bit of flattened grass? It's scandalous." As he shuffled forward with the queue, he moaned on, "I wonder how much the lavatories cost this year. It'll be at least a pound, so if you're gonna use 'em, make sure you get your money's worth."

Ten minutes later, Simon pulled into the field ahead of us, Dennis followed and immediately went into full moan mode again as the car bumped and buffeted on the uneven ground. "All this bumping about won't do her suspension any favours."

Strangers might be tempted to think he meant suspenders and that he'd seen some elderly woman struggling to keep her stockings in place. In fact, he was talking about his precious car. It was the light of his life and he treated it with reverence and gentility that sometimes made me envious. If he showed me the same level of tenderness and consideration, I'd flag him up as the perfect husband.

"Yeah, but if I was perfect, I wouldn't need you, would I?" was his usual response to the proposition.

As we neared the pay point, manned by two men in official, council hi-vis safety vests, Dennis patted his pockets. "Lend us a fiver, Chrissy. I can't find my wallet."

I tutted and dug into my purse. "Is it true what Lester Grimes says about you? The last time you bought a round was the night Leeds United won the FA Cup."

"Not true," he replied, taking the five pound note from me. "That was in 1972, and I was only about three year old."

"Perhaps he meant Manchester United then."

"No way would I buy a round for Manchester United winning the cup."

Once he paid the fee, he followed Simon into the parking area, but while our son shuffled his Citroen into a convenient spot near the coin slot portaloos, Dennis refused, and backed into a space opposite. "I'm not leaving her in front of the lavatories," he declared as he shut down the engine and climbed out.

I followed him out into the warm sunshine. "Make sure you've got your wallet, Dennis."

He patted his back pocket. "I've got it."

I held out my hand. "Good. Then open it and give me back my five pounds." As he handed the money over, I reminded him, "I have people I need to speak to so I may have to leave you with Simon and Naomi for a while. And hey, don't leave them paying for the rides for Bethany. We can afford it better than them."

"I can see this is gonna be an expensive afternoon."

"It could be worse. Have you seen the prices on Central Pier in Blackpool?"

"No, but I'll bear it in mind next time we go to Blacky."

Linking up with Simon and Naomi, we followed the crowds along the broad, roped off path to the actual fairground, Bethany skipping along, holding my hand and her mother's while Dennis and Simon followed a couple of yards behind. We could hear the music from the rides, and I could see the spire of the Helter Skelter, and the carriage of the slingshot flying into the air, and I felt again a distant reminder of the excitement the fair had brought to my much younger self.

We passed along through the gap in the line of trees and bushes and the fairground opened up before us. As I anticipated, it was packed with visitors, most of them casually dressed, welcoming the spring sun on their bare arms, and for those wearing shorts, their bare legs. The smell of candy floss, brandy snap, and more modern fast foods, hot dogs, burgers, the inevitable chips permeated the air, and as a backdrop to music so loud it was almost incomprehensible, came the thrum of diesel engines working to power the attractions. Off to one side, music pounded from the speakers of the various rides, and directly opposite we could hear the crack of rifles and ting of an occasional bullseye on Singer's shooting gallery. From beyond it came the siren warning that a dodgems session was about to start.

Bethany's greedy eyes settled on the teacup ride, and I directed Dennis to the pay kiosk where they had to purchase tickets for the rides. Aside from the food stalls, every ride, every attraction cost a minimum of two tickets, and some were as expensive as five, so I instructed my husband to buy a book of at least twenty-five tickets, which would set him back twenty pounds.

"It's for that child," I said, when he almost fainted. "If I can't spoil her, who can I spoil?"

"Well you could start with me," he grumbled and moved off to buy the tickets.

I took the opportunity to appraise Simon of my plans. "I'll sit with Bethany on the teacups, but then I'll have to leave you for a while."

"You're not the only one. I'm on duty, remember. I'll have to leave Nam and Beth with Dad."

"Your father will cope... well, he'd better. And your wife is Naomi and you christened your daughter Bethany."

Naomi moved to defend her husband. "I don't mind, Chrissy. Honestly. I get annoyed sometimes that my mum lumbered me with a name like Naomi."

"Parents are like that, Naomi, and you should honour their wishes."

At that moment a black and white missile hurtled in towards us, and it was only when I heard George Ibble shouting, "Come here, you little sodpot," that I realised the incoming Scud missile was Banjo.

Simon and Naomi had no pets. They had enough on their hands with a hyperactive three-year-old. As a result, when Banjo came bounding, Bethany took instant alarm and cowered behind her mother.

Banjo fussed and wagged his tail, and I patted him on the head. "Hello, Banjo. Are you having fun?" I beamed on Bethany. "It's only Banjo. He won't hurt you. He just wants to play." I soothed the dog again. "Don't you, boy?" As I stroked his ears, the oscillation of his tail increased. He looked up at me, eyes beaming pure love, mouth open, panting in the heat, begging me to feed him.

George arrived. "Hello, Chrissy. Listen, I'm sorry, lass. He's been a pain in the posterior all morning." He slipped a leash over the dog's head and round his neck, and waved at the crowds again. "It's all these people. He thinks they've all come out to play with him."

I tried to disapprove but I couldn't help laughing. "He scared the living daylights out of my granddaughter."

George chuckled and spoke to Bethany. "He won't hurt you, chicken. He's like you. A little boy and all he wants to do is play."

I dropped the idea of disapproval and smiled again as Bethany crept forward and tapped Banjo on the nose with her tiny hand. The dog licked her fingers in a show of instant friendship.

"How did he do in the obedience class, George?"

"It hasn't happened yet. We're on the field at half past two. I'm dreading it, Chrissy. It doesn't matter how many treats I offer, his attention still wanders." He frowned. "His appetite's not what it should be, either. I'm wondering if some of my competitors are feeding him behind my back. Y'see, the hungrier he is, the more he'll pay attention, and everyone knows how many times I've been a winner up and down the country."

Simon butted in. "Sabotage at the dog show? Sounds like a job for Mam."

"I have enough on, thank you, Simon." I focussed on George to bring the discussion to an end. "Let us know how Banjo gets on," I insisted with that level of insincerity which said I didn't really care.

"Oh, I know how he'll get on. I'll see you around, Chrissy, Simon." With a polite nod to Naomi, George dragged Banjo off.

Dennis returned with the tickets, and I led Bethany to the teacup ride where we spent a calming five minutes going round in circles.

As the ride went round, the view passed the waltzers and the dodgems, my eye fell on Sandra's van, and she had a sizeable queue waiting to be fed and watered. By the time our teacup had gone round one more time, George Ibble and Banjo had joined the queue and people were fussing over the dog. Judging by the speed with which his tail was wagging, Banjo must have been creating a noticeable draft.

Dennis had always preferred dogs, but when we first got together I persuaded him towards cats. If nothing else, dogs needed walking a couple of times a day. Cappy the Cat only needed the door opening and he could do as he wished. Come to think, our moggie was master of his own destiny and did as he wished, whether the doors were open or otherwise.

When the ride came to a stop, Bethany and I climbed off and I handed her over to her parents, and she gave her mother a breathless account of the last five minutes as only a child of three, still mastering the English language, could. "Me and Nan (large intake of breath) Na on the teak (large intake of breath) ups."

Dennis was sulking, which I recognised as an urgent desire to take in the splendour of the Gardner engines, so I told him that Simon and I had work to do and he would be left with Naomi and Bethany. That only deepened his sulks. Instructing him to keep his phone switched on I took my leave of them and went in search of some of my targets.

The first was the closest but not necessarily the easiest to pin down. Jim Singer, still operating only five of his six guns, had called a halt to the shooting while he replaced the paper targets. He already had a full house of punters waiting to demonstrate their crackshot capabilities, and to look at them it seemed obvious to me that to a man – and one woman – they were so convinced of their skills that they would have the police ARU training school tripping over its collective DMS boots to sign them up.

I waited patiently at one end of the stall, the end where I had seen Singer stand while the customers were blowing the heads off imaginary terrorists in the shape of tiny metal ducks. And while I waited, looked around. I could see Dennis looking bored but waving to Bethany when she and Naomi came past on one of the children's gentler rides. I saw Gina Kilsby walking towards the ticket booth, and she looked back at me, then change her mind and made her way hurriedly back to the accommodation vans.

What, I asked myself, had I done now to generate her suspicion?

"Fancy yourself as duck a hunter, do you, luv?" Singer asked having returned to stand away from the anticipated fusillade. He held out a hand for my tickets.

"I thought you might remember me from yesterday when you were complaining to my son, the police detective, about your missing rifle. I don't fancy myself for hunting ducks. I fancy myself as a private investigator and I'm making inquiries into the death of Frank Kilsby."

"I don't know nothing about it, missis."

"About what? Kilsby's death or your missing gun?"

"Now listen—"

Why did everyone start with that kind of instruction? He was speaking loud enough to drown out the cacophony of alleged music blaring all around us, and since I was here to question him I had no choice but to listen.

"No, you listen," I interrupted. "Frank hired me to find out who was threatening him. Twenty-four hours later, he was dead, and he had a wound on his temple from a BB pellet, one of your BB pellets. I've given this a lot of thought and there is no way, Mr Singer, no way at all that one of your rifles could have disappeared in crowds like this without someone noticing. I have some simple questions to which I'd prefer honest answers. If I don't get them,

I'll call the police in again and they'll shut you down until they get those answers. Someone either paid or threatened you to hand over one of your guns. Who was it?"

"No one." He shrugged. "You wanted simple answers."

"I also want honest answers, and I don't believe you. Reporting that rifle stolen was a red herring, designed to blindside the police. I want the truth, and my son is here. I either get the truth or I call him in now, and he won't be half as gentle as me."

Singer huffed out is breath. "If this is you being gentle, I wouldn't like to meet you in a paddy."

"Yes well, talking of Paddy, have you met DI Quinn? His name is Patrick and we all know him as Paddy, and he usually takes a can opener to his suspects' heads. He says it gives him direct access to their brains. The truth, Mr Singer."

This time, it was a long sigh of resignation. He was saved by three of the five shooters running out of ammunition. He held up a hand to stop the shooting, collected and replaced the targets, handed over the necessary win vouchers to those who had earned them, and then came back to me. The look on his face said he wished I'd disappeared while he attended to his customers and I was happy to disappoint him. In order to stress the point, I put on my most severe face, the one I used when I needed to pull Dennis into line.

"Right. The truth. See, what actually happened was, when I was setting up yesterday, the rifle had already gone, and since we didn't have no punters on Thursday, it had to be one of the crew."

"Well, why didn't you tell Simon that?"

He shrugged. "Haven't you already been told? We're fairground folk. We have our own way of dealing with the scroats, so I wasn't about to say nothing, but that copper, your son is he, well, he noticed and started asking questions."

"You're saying Simon approached you and not the other way about?"

"That's how it happened."

I reminded myself to have a word with Simon. "And has the rifle turned up?"

"Nope. The cops were searching the river yesterday, but word is they didn't find it. Ten to one, whoever nicked it, they've already hawked it off in the town."

"After shooting Frank Kilsby in the head with it. Prime suspect?"

"Yeah. It was a serial on the telly about thirty years ago."

He said it with an insouciant grin and that was a prompt for me to deliver the serious face again. "The truth, Singer. Who's the most likely candidate?"

Another shrug. "Coulda been anybody. We have our rules and nicking is against them, but that don't stop it happening. I'll tell you what, though, Gina was off into town on her Yammy the other day."

The bells rang in my head. Was that why she turned back towards her van when she saw me waiting to speak to Singer?

The stallholder gave me another grin, slyer this time. "But I don't reckon your chances of getting anything out of her except a mouthful."

Chapter Sixteen

I'm not naturally ill-tempered. I take most of what life throws at me in my stride, but there are exceptions.

Look at the time I was in hospital for, ahem, a woman's problem, and Dennis decided to help me by dealing with the week's laundry. From a technical point of view, I can't fault him. When we first bought the washing machine, he fitted it, plumbed in all the pipes, built it into kitchen units perfectly. I couldn't be happier with the job he did for me. But he never learned how to use it. He left that end of things to me, and I was fine with the arrangement. While I was in hospital for the day, he decided he would become the perfect husband and deal with the weekly wash. As I recall, he was actually sweetening me up because he wanted an eight-track stereo to fit into his Morris Marina and as a retro item, they could be quite expensive.

But he didn't bother sorting the washing, just crammed as much as he could into the machine and set it going. Even Cappy the Cat realised something was wrong when my lambswool cardigan came out small enough to fit Bethany, and its delicate shade of pink was now a delicate shade of puce grey... perfectly matching the shade of my white knickers.

And the less said about the white bed sheets and his navy blue underpants the better. They looked well-matched when I cut them up for rags. He never did get that eight-track. The money which would have paid for it went on replacing the damaged clothing and bed linen.

With that in mind, I came away from the shooting gallery with my mood varying between irritable to mildly satisfied on a basis of better informed. I needed a quick word with Simon to confirm (or otherwise) Singer's story, and I needed a sterner word with Gina Kilsby. But that mood soon rose to Dennis and the week's washing anger when I saw Gina, clad in her black and red leathers, weave her way through the crowds on her Yamaha. I would have hurried in pursuit, but there was no point. My car was at home, and even if I could find him and get the keys, Dennis's Morris would never catch her.

That girl, as I had always suspected, knew more than she was letting on. She also knew that Singer would bow to pressure and that I would be looking for her after speaking to him.

I marched to the ticket booth, but the queue was too long for me to insist that Rachel break off and speak to me. Instead, as I had done the previous day, I left her a note telling her I needed to speak to her urgently, and then turned for the accommodation vans.

I didn't get further than ten yards when Madame Márta Mitrea pulled me up. "You would like me to tell your fortune for the feast of Walpurgis?" Her voice carried a thick, east European lilt which only inflamed my temper.

"No I would not. I don't celebrate Walpurgis. And you can drop the phoney accent. Frank Kilsby told me you come from Runcorn, and you've never been closer to Rumania than the promenade at Bridlington."

She tutted. "You're that private eye who's been poking around, aren't you?" Her accent was gone, replaced by her semi-scouse brogue. When I nodded, she said, "Yes, well, he's got a big mouth, that Frank."

"Had a big mouth. He's dead, remember. Was that the only thing big about him, Martha?"

The fiery eyes blazed. "Whaddya mean?" Her accent, like a loose weathervane, had wandered in the direction of New York.

"Well, according to the whispers, you saw quite a lot of him. All of him, in fact, and mostly horizontal, if the tales are to be believed."

Her shoulders fell. "And you think I was the only one? He had most of the women working this fair, and some that he shouldn't have had. Ask Heidi Dodds on the hook-a-duck stand. By all accounts Frank was the father of her kid, and she was married at the time."

"I'll get to her. Do you know why he called me in?" I asked, and didn't wait for an answer. "Because he received a note saying he wouldn't live to see Walpurgis. Now how many people on this fair know about Walpurgis?"

"Who's to say it's someone from the crew?"

"Me, that's who. And I know it's someone from the crew."

"If you say so. It wasn't me." The fake Rumanian accent came back. "And as it happens, dollink, I'm the only one who celebrates Walpurgis."

"With an orgy?"

"A gross distortion of the true meaning of Walpurgis. There are no orgies."

"Not with Frank gone. Tell me something, Martha, is every member of the crew here eccentric?"

I detected evil or at least mischief in her smile. "Well, it helps."

I would get no sense out of her, so I went in search of Simon and found him with his father, both watching Naomi with Bethany on our granddaughter's second ride on the teacups. Like a dutiful grandparent, Dennis was videoing the child who waved every time she came round. I drew Simon to one side and asked about his interlude with Singer. He confirmed that he had approached the stallholder, but he was a little miffed when I told him what Singer had told me about the rifle going missing overnight.

"Blooming typical. How are we supposed to work out what's happening when they don't tell us the truth? I meanersay, if he'd told me that, Mandy probably wouldn't have bothered searching the river. I'd better have a word with Gina."

"Difficult," I said, and told him how she'd ridden off on her motorcycle. "She saw me talking to Singer, he suggested she might be responsible, and then she took off. Even if she didn't steal the rifle, I'm willing to bet she knows something about it."

"She won't have gone far, Mam. She lives here." He gave me his fondest smile. "I have to say, you've really got the bit between your teeth on this one, haven't you?"

"I've been paid a lot of money to sort it out, Simon, and I won't let go."

He nodded past me. "You might have to."

I turned to look in the direction he indicated by his concerned eyes and there was Paddy Quinn bearing down on us, Mandy struggling to keep up with him. And Paddy didn't look as if he wanted to join my fan club.

"Inspector Quinn—"

"Shut it, Capper." Having cut me off, he focussed on Simon first. "I thought I told you to keep her out of this case."

"Sir, I—"

I interrupted before Simon could go any further. "For your information, Inspector, I am here for a day out with my family; my husband, son, daughter-in-law and granddaughter."

"Tell me anoth—"

I cut Quinn off this time. "And as for telling Simon that I should keep out of Frank Kilsby's murder, he was a bona fide client and as long as I'm not interfering with your investigation there's nothing you can do about it. To go further, everything I've learned, I've passed on to Simon or Detective Sergeant Hiscoe. And in future, you might find me better tempered if you address me as Christine or Mrs Capper, rather than Capper. I hope I've made myself clear."

Getting Paddy Quinn to back down was not as

simple as that. "You have, but I'm warning you, overstep the mark and I'll throw you in the cells. Understand?"

"Perfectly."

I wasn't willing to let things go at that. I knew Paddy Quinn of old. He was on the beat when I was a probationer, and even back then, he would use any kind of leverage to get what he wanted. I wouldn't put it past him to hold Simon back as a means of applying pressure to me, and a complaint to his superintendent would only produce a string of denials from Paddy, and even more pressure on my son.

Conversely, because I'd known him so long, I knew a lot about him, probably more than he would like me to know, and as something of a very minor celebrity in Haxford (it's true. My vlog took 1,000 or more hits a week) I had an above average level of influence.

"There's just one last thing, Mr Quinn. Police discipline is nothing to do with me, but if I hear of you taking out my attitude on my son, or threatening to hold him back because I won't toe your line, I might be tempted to let my vlog viewers and blog readers know what you get up when you spend all that time in the gents lavatories."

He turned several shades of crimson, snapped his fingers at Mandy and marched off. She followed with a resigned shrug at me.

Dennis had watched the exchange with interest. "What does he get up to in the gents toilets," he asked as we watched them storm away.

"Who knows and who cares. It shut him up,

didn't it? Considering his stress levels, maybe he's suffering from IBS." I faced my son. "If he gives you any grief, Simon, you let me know."

Barely able to suppress his humour, my son shook his head. "I can handle him myself, Mam, once they make me a full DC." His face fell again. "If ever."

I was at a slight loss for a suitable direction. Rachel had not yet seen fit to respond to my note (too soon after receiving it and too busy) and if Gina had sneaked back in (unlikely) Paddy and Mandy would buttonhole her. Ossie was a possibility, but a glance over the tops of various rides told me that the slingshot was in operation and I guessed there would be a huge queue and he would be too busy to talk to me. Madame Márta had proven a waste of my time, so it might just be time to have a brief word with Heidi on the hook-a-duck stall, another of Kilsby's alleged conquests.

And then I noticed the forty-something with the straggly, dark brown hair operating the teacups. Her head was buried in a celebrity magazine and she wasn't taking much notice of the ride. I don't know how many times Naomi and Bethany had gone round, but although Naomi was looking bored, Bethany was loving every minute of it, still waving to her dad, Dennis, and me as she passed.

I made my way round to the booth. And rapped on the door.

"Yes?"

She said it as if I'd asked a question rather than her asking what did I want, and I was tempted to respond, "Thanks. That's good to know," but she didn't look like the brightest star in the firmament, and I didn't want to confuse her before we got down to serious business.

I consulted the staff list lodged in my head. "It's Pauline, isn't it?"

"Who wants to know?"

"Christine Capper. I'm the private investigator looking into the threats made against Frank before he died."

"I don't know nothing."

I refrained from pointing out that the double negative actually meant a positive i.e. that she did know something, and instead, said, "You knew Frank, though, didn't you?"

"Everybody knew Frank. Wonderful man. This place wouldn't exist without him."

I charitably assumed she meant the fair and not Barncroft's Meadow. Then again, maybe she did mean Barncroft's Meadow. The look on her face when she said it meant she considered Kilsby somewhere close to God if not the actual incarnation of the almighty.

"He always made sure I got a prime spot no matter where we're standing," she concluded.

"You know, you're the first person I've spoken to who had anything good to say about him. From that, I assume you had an affair with him too."

"Hardly an affair." She wasn't the slightest bit defensive. "We had our moments."

"Was he drunk at the time?"

I didn't mean to say it. The thought was at the front of my mind that the Kilsby I knew so briefly wouldn't look twice at an overweight, untidy gargoyle like this.

Now she was defensive. "I haven't always looked like this, you know."

No, I thought. I bet you've run a comb through your stringy mop a time or two.

"You wanna know who kilt him, look at that little tart, Gina, or Rache. Neither of 'em never had nowt good to say about him."

This time, I couldn't work out what the plethora of negatives added up to.

"All right. Thanks. Just one last thing?"

"What?"

I pointed through her booth to the ride. "How many more times are you gonna let the teacups go round? Only my daughter-in-law's looking a bit cheesed off."

I joined Simon and Dennis again as the ride came to a stop and Naomi and Bethany climbed off. Bethany proceeded to give me a blow by blow account of her excitement while the world went past her, but I was more concentrated on a furious Paddy Quinn hurtling towards me.

"Where is she, Capper?"

I was flummoxed. "What are you talking about?"

"Kilsby's girl? The biker. You warned her, didn't you, and she's taken off on her bike."

"Don't talk daft. I wanted to speak to her myself but she was gone before I could get there."

"And I don't believe you, you…"

Chapter Seventeen

"Hey. Don't you talk to my missus like that."

Dennis's interruption came in the nick of time, cutting off a tirade of abuse before Quinn could verbalise it.

I'll say this for my husband, he always had serious bottle. He stood about five feet eleven, and although he was in his early fifties, his heavy job of work kept him fit and muscular. If he were not so obsessed by all things mechanical he would have been a dreamboat for any woman. And he was even tempered, but in all the years we had been together, he had never allowed any man to talk down to or curse me. Women, yes, but not men. He was never any use arguing with a determined woman.

When he cut in, Paddy gave him the full glare, so hot it was practically dazzling. "Do you know who I am?"

"Course I do," Dennis replied. "And even if I didn't, you're shouting loud enough for everyone to guess. And I don't care who you are or what you are. You wanna talk to my wife you keep a civil tongue in your head."

Quinn pointed a shaking finger at me while talking to Dennis. "She told a suspect to get out of here because we wanted to speak to her."

"Did she h—"

"Dennis!"

"—eck as like. She hasn't spoken to anyone this afternoon except that barmpot fortune teller."

"And Singer on the shooting gallery," I said, "and Pauline who runs the teacups." It took a millisecond for me to realise I was helping dig my own grave, so I switched tactics. "And how do you imagine I'd know you'd wanted to speak to Gina?"

Quinn did not answer. Instead, he switched his glower to Simon.

"Wrong, sir," my son said. Say what you like about us Cappers, but we're more than willing to fight our corner against your common or garden despot. "For one thing, I didn't know you wanted to speak to Gina Kilsby, so I couldn't have told Mam, and if I had known, I still wouldn't have said anything to her."

"You should be thinking about your career, lad. It—"

"Sir." This time it was Mandy who cut off Quinn's attempted rant. "Just calm down a bit, and let's go back to the car and have a quiet word."

Going back to the car for a 'quiet word' was police euphemism for a junior officer, such as Mandy, ripping her boss to pieces. She would not do it in public to avoid making him look a bigger fool than he had already achieved off his own bat.

The blazing eyes swung again, to settle on me. "I won't forget this, Capper."

"Mrs Capper to you, Quinn," I said to his departing back.

With them gone, Simon turned a disapproving

eye on me. "Did you tell her the police were looking for her?"

"No, I did not. As I've just said to that idiot, I didn't know. And I told you what happened when I went looking for her, and I may lie to your father now and then, but I don't lie to you or the police in general."

Dennis's brow furrowed. "What do you lie to me about?"

"You really don't want to know, luv. Now come, all of you. I think it's time this child was having something to eat and I need a cup of tea."

Bethany's eyes lit up. "I (large intake of breath) scream?"

"Yes, lovey. You can have an ice cream."

After furnishing the child with a 99, we made our way to Sandra's van where I laid eyes on the huge queue, then made for the back door and managed to secure our order, four teas, two cheeseburgers and fries (Dennis and Simon) two medium fries (Naomi and me) and while Dennis and I wondered when and why they stopped calling them chips, we perched on Sandra's bread trays looking north towards the show ring and enjoying the afternoon sunshine.

Once finished with her ice cream – I swear I had never seen a child demolish a medium sized cone topped with ice cream and a chocolate flake so quickly – and suffered the ignominy of her mother running a tissue over her smeared face, Bethany shared the fries with Naomi and me, and my memory of the previous day had me scanning the fields, looking for George and Banjo. At the far end

I could see the crowds surrounding the show area and we caught occasional muted ripples of applause.

"Banjo?" Dennis asked when I mentioned it. "Who in the name of power screwdrivers is Banjo?"

"George Ibble's new dog. He's still a pup and George is trying to train him."

"Oh. Right. And what have you been lying to me about?"

"Later, Dennis. When we're home on our own."

Simon laughed. "Have you got another bloke on the side, Mam?"

Naomi clucked. "Men. They're all the same. One track minds."

"Which is why one man is enough for me, Naomi."

"If anyone's cheating in our house, it's Chrissy," Dennis said.

I groaned. I knew what was coming.

Naomi tried unsuccessfully to bury her shock. "Dennis, that's a serious accusation."

"But true," my old man went on. "She insisted on a French car. What's that if it's not treason."

I made an effort to educate my daughter-in-law. "It's an old argument, luv. Dennis talking out of his backside."

He rose to the challenge. "What's wrong with British cars?"

"As far as I'm aware, Ford and Vauxhall are both American," I said, "Jaguar and Land Rover belonged to Tata Motors, who are based in Mumbai, British Leyland and Reliant have been history for decades, which leaves us with Aston Martin, and even if they are still British, which I'm not one hundred percent certain of, I don't think we could afford one."

Mandy appeared. How she found us, I don't know, but it was reasonable to assume she asked Sandra. Right on cue, the woman herself came out with a cup of tea for our friendly detective sergeant.

"Has Quinn calmed down?" I asked.

"Not so you'd notice. I told him what a prat he was making of himself, and how it was impossible for you or Simon to warn Gina off because the reason we want to speak to her only became apparent an hour ago."

"And what is the reason? Or is that classified, for the eyes and ears of Paddy Quinn's inner circle only?"

"He's not here, Chrissy. He's gone back to Huddersfield. He'll give his wife some verbal tonight and if I know Janine, she'll rip him to bits."

I compelled her to focus. "The reason you're looking for Gina?"

"The CCTV footage from inside the ghost train. There's a good fifteen, twenty minutes of it missing, and it's critical. It's around the time Frank Kilsby went in. The screen goes blank as Frank comes round the track to see to the puppet, and when it starts up again, he's on his back and the car is coming straight at him."

"The critical bit was deliberately cut out?" I asked.

"It's almost impossible for it to be otherwise, Chrissy," Naomi said.

I'd never really known what it was she studied at

university or what she did for a living before she moved to Haxford. I know it was something to do with information technology and that included video processing.

I raised my eyebrows at her and she went on to explain.

"Unless there's direct interference with it, CCTV will record continuously. And if Mandy is right, then you have to say that someone downloaded the video, cut that section out and then saved it again."

"But they didn't remove the timestamp," Mandy confirmed, "and it's that timestamp which tells us there's a sizable chunk missing. Since Gina gave us the recording on a memory stick, she's the prime suspect, and we have to talk to her."

I handed the remainder of my fries to Bethany, and wiped my hands on a tissue. "Well, it's nothing to do with me, Mandy." I went on to tell her what had happened after I spoke to Singer.

"It looks as if she had even more to hide," Simon chipped in. "I mean, how would Singer know that a section of the CCTV recording was missing? Mam was speaking to him about his missing gun. So does Gina know something about that too?"

The discussion never went any further. A black and white bundle came gambolling down the hill, mouth open, tail ready to shift into overdrive and a few seconds later, Banjo was fussing between us. Some distance behind him, George looked out of breath.

"Oh, crikey, I'm sorry, Chrissy, Dennis," he said when he caught up with his pet tearaway. "The little swine got away from me."

Bethany was braver this time, and when Banjo came to her, she offered him a chip. He declined, and began sniffing round Simon's upper legs, but I got the impression he was more interested in the bread trays than my son.

"How did he do in the show, George?" I asked.

"No worse than the average catastrophe. When it comes to obedience, he does as he pleases. Tell him to sit and he lies down, rolls onto his back and if you're not quick enough, he's asleep in seconds. And agility? I've had this dog since birth, and I've never seen him so tired. I'm telling you, someone has been feeding him while my back's turned. He's not like this at home. I mean, just now, he only livened up when he saw you lot sitting here."

Right now, Banjo was ignoring us and trying desperately to get to the bread trays while Simon kept pushing him back.

And that's when I made the connection. "Oh dear."

All eyes locked onto me as I knocked on the door.

"What's up, Chrissy," Sandra asked. "Do you want more tea, or summat? Only we're very busy."

Banjo's reaction to her was interesting and confirmed my suspicion. He forgot the bread trays, sat obediently before her, his begging eyes beaming into her. It was almost as if he knew that Sandra was the supplier of all those lovely buns.

She smiled down at him. "Cracking little fella, George."

"A pain in the buttock, Sandra."

"He's also your mystery bun thief," I declared,

and I was once again the centre of attention. "George, you said he only perked up when he saw us. Are you sure he wasn't focussed on Sandra's van?"

"Well, I, er…" George pushed his cap back and scratched his forehead. "Well, he has legged it down here quite a few times over the last couple of days. What are you saying, Chrissy?"

"Sandra has been missing some freshly baked buns over the last two days, and you say someone has been feeding Banjo. Whoever was taking the buns didn't steal the whole tray. Just two or three, and without asking Sandra, I'll bet those three were from the outside edge of the tray, not the middle. I imagine they'd be enough to fill Banjo's young belly. You think someone has been feeding him to scotch your chances in the show, but in fact, no one has been feeding him. He's been helping himself."

George's face, already bright red with exertion, defied chemistry and turned even redder. "Oh, my God. I'm so sorry, Sandra."

I waited for her to explode, but she didn't. Instead, she laughed out loud, stepped down from the van, and patted the dog's head. "Have you been nicking my best buns, you little beggar."

Banjo responded by wagging his tail even faster.

"Naturally, I'll pay for them," George offered.

"Ah, don't bother, George. It's only a few quid, and you should know that I'm a sucker for dogs. They're more reliable than people." She pulled open the door again, and shouted, "Alice, chuck me a sausage roll, will you, I've a hungry collie out here."

Her sister delivered, and Sandra sat on the step, breaking off bits of the sausage roll and feeding Banjo. "You don't mind, do you, George?"

"Even if I did I wouldn't say so, but watch him. He's a still a teenager in dog terms, and he'll eat you out of house and home."

Sandra laughed again, and continued to feed Banjo, and I was impressed with the dog's patience. He didn't demand and when offered the food, he didn't snatch.

She eyed me. "I suppose you want paying now, do you?"

I shook my head. "Forget it, Sandra. You've been more than generous to George and his dog, so I can be generous to you. Besides, you've been supplying free tea for the last two days, and to be honest, I only made the connection because we happened to be here when Banjo came running. If we hadn't been here, I would probably never have guessed."

Sat before Sandra, Banjo couldn't understand why he was suddenly the centre of everyone's attention. Not that he cared. He was too focussed on the sausage roll.

Chapter Eighteen

With the excitement over, we ambled further into the fair. Dennis disappeared to check out the engines driving the dodgems and waltzer, Bethany began to get sleepy and before long, Simon was carrying her.

"We should have brought her trolley," Naomi said.

Simon promptly agreed to take his daughter back to the car where she could sleep for a while. Naomi offered to stay with me, but I told her to go with her husband. I had other matters I needed to attend to. While they wandered off, I rang Dennis and appraised him of the situation, and he said it was time we were thinking about going home.

"Fine. You get off home and when I'm through with my investigation, I'll call you to come and pick me up."

"Yeah, but that noddy on the gate'll charge me another fiver."

"It's either that or you hang around, Dennis," I said and cut the call before he could protest any further.

I still hadn't seen anything of Rachel, and when I checked the accommodation vans there was no sign of Gina's Yamaha, and nor could I see Kaiser. The dog was probably locked up in the van, and along with the missing bike, I took that as a sign that she wasn't back either. The only person in evidence was young Nick, and he was busy preparing a sign, on a large sheet of white cardboard. He was using a red marker, and as he worked on the lettering, his tongue followed the track of the pen across the board.

"Hello, Nick. Is your mother around?"

He looked up. "No. Dunno where she is. Her bike's not here, so she's gone off somewhere."

"Leaving you holding the fort, eh?"

He frowned. "We haven't got no fort. And I've no work to do cos the ghost train's shut. That's what I'm doing. Getting a sign ready to tell people it's shut. Cos me granddad's dead, y'know. Got run over in the ghost train and the scuffers made us shut it."

That was the second time I'd heard the word 'scuffers' in the last three days. A genuine merseysider, this boy, and his matter-of-fact account spelled out a simple young man who accepted the world around him with all its foibles, triumphs, and disasters as no more than background noise to his uncomplicated life.

"How do you feel about that, Nick? Your granddad being dead?"

He shrugged. "He were all right sometimes, but mostly he were mean. Bad. Y'know. Nobody liked him, excepting Pauline as what runs the kids' rides, but they'd been doing stuff in her van. Grown up stuff."

I didn't need any clarification on that point so I

drifted sideways. "Why didn't they like him?"

"Cos he used to thump 'em when they didn't do as they're told. He used to thump me an'all. I didn't always like him, specially when he did that."

"I can understand. Was there—"

"What do you want, woman? Haven't we seen enough of you?"

I turned to meet Rachel's voice. As always she was in a spat. I don't think I'd seen her smile since I met her, except when she was with Ossie.

"I've been all over this fair looking for you," she ranted. "You left a note and I couldn't find you."

After three days of it, I was beginning to tire of this woman's bile, and it was never a good idea to confront Christine Capper when she was that way out. I met her virulence with some of my own. "I've been busy, Mrs Kilsby. Busy looking for your daughter. And I'm not alone. The police are looking for her, too. She has questions to answer. Now where is she?"

"How the hell should I know? And she's not my daughter. She's my stepdaughter, and she's thirty years old. She's not answerable to me. Even when she was younger she wasn't, and she wouldn't take any notice of her dad."

"Did you people ever learn the meaning of the words parental responsibility? Did you never drill any discipline into her when she was a child."

"Ask Frank. She's his brat."

"A bit difficult since he's no longer with us. I want to know what she knows about the air rifle stolen from Jim Singer's stall."

"Nothing, likely as not. And before you ask, I

don't know anything, either, so why don't you just clear off and leave us alone?"

"When I've learned what happened to Frank, I will."

"Who cares what happened to him."

How could she say such a thing? The term 'marriage of convenience' had never meant much to me. In Haxford, most people married because there was some feeling between them, some emotional attachment. Rachel had obviously married Kilsby purely for the level of security he could bring to her and beyond that, she had no interest in him.

It dawned on me that, based on Ossie's testimony, Frank Kilsby must have felt the same way. He married her for nothing more than her sexual favours and (perhaps) her housekeeping skills, although, memories of the state of her caravan soon cast doubt on that.

It also penetrated my sometimes dim awareness, that my failure to understand probably had more to do with my comfortable marriage and a total lack of wisdom regarding the modern world.

Be that as it may, the callous disregard for her husband and his fate prompted my annoyance to climb another couple of points. "I care, Mrs Kilsby, and I'm determined to get to the truth. Until I do, get used to me. I'm not going away."

In what must have seemed like a contradiction to my last words, I performed a smart about turn, the way they taught us in police training college, and marched away.

I was absolutely furious with Rachel, and Gina, and Ossie, and all the other fairground folk. It was as if protecting their own community was worth more than this man's life. And then I recalled something at least one of them had said to me on Thursday or was it Friday? "You're a townie, an outsider. No one will talk to you." And yet people had talked to me. I'd managed to breach their wall of silence. I took some pride from that and all I had to do to increase that level of communication was apply more pressure, turn on the hard act again.

Consequently, as I made my way back through the fairground and I saw Gina coming towards me, I stood my ground.

She was moving slowly, weaving through the crowds, but when she came across small, open spaces, she accelerated a little. It was on the edge of one of those spaces that I faced her and held up my hand. She swerved to go round me, and I moved to block the way. She swerved the other way and I moved again. She revved the machine and came straight at me. For a moment I thought she was going to run me down, but yards from me, she hit the brakes, dropped one foot on the ground to support herself and the bike, switched off the engine, and removed her helmet.

"Are you totally out of your tree?"

The volume of her question made us the centre of attention for a few moments.

Conscious of so many eyes on me, I had two choices. Run for it or stand my ground. It was a no brainer. "I need to speak to you."

"Well, I've nothing to say."

"Then you'd better find something because the police are looking for you, and Paddy Quinn wasn't in the best of moods last time I saw him."

"I can't tell you anything."

"Yes you can. You can tell me why you were on your way to the ticket booth earlier after I'd insisted on speaking to Rachel, and why you changed your mind when you saw me talking to Jim Singer, and climbed on your motorbike to get away from me."

"I don't—"

I cut in before she could complete her excuse. "And while you're at it, you can tell me why you cut out a large chunk out of the CCTV recording which showed what happened to Frank."

"I didn't."

Most of the crowd had dispersed, but her denial was delivered in a high-pitched voice protesting such innocence that they turned again to watch the unfolding argument.

Looking over Gina's shoulder, I could see Mandy making her way towards us, and right behind her was Simon. I focused on the motorcycle madam and finally responded to her protest. "You'd better tell that to the police because they're here to arrest you."

She glanced over her shoulder and her face fell. "Oh, for crying out loud..." she turned back to face me. "None of this is anything to do with me."

"Then start talking, Gina, because if you don't you're going to be looking at a prison sentence."

"Gina Kilsby," a breathless Mandy said as she caught up with us, "I'm arresting you on suspicion of attempting to pervert the course of justice by withholding evidence pertaining to the death of Frank Kilsby, and of tampering with that evidence. I must caution you—"

"Yeah, yeah, I've heard it all before, but you've got it wrong. Listen, can I get the bike back to my van and we can talk there?"

"You're going to the police station."

"But I haven't done anything."

If asked, I would freely admit that I didn't care for this girl and her blasé attitude to the world around her, but something told me she was telling the truth. "I'd listen first, if I were you, Mandy," I suggested. "Not up to me to tell you how to do your job, of course, but…"

She thought about it for a moment and held out her hand. "Keys for the bike," she insisted, and backed it up with a sadistic smile. "Just so you don't try to do a runner."

With a resigned 'hmpf' Gina handed over the key and with the crowds still focussed on us, pushed the bike along as we walked back to the accommodation area.

When we got there, she propped the bike on its stand, and unlocked the door. Leading us in, she commented. "Don't know where Nick's got to."

"He was making a sign confirming the ghost train was closed when I was with him earlier," I said.

"He was supposed to do that yesterday. Listen, does one of you want to make us all a brew while I get my leathers off?"

Mandy nodded at Simon who attended to the kettle while Gina disappeared into the back of the van.

The place was as unkempt and untidy as her

stepmother's next door and again I felt that urge to flit home and come back with my cleaning gear. I'd never considered myself particularly houseproud, but I couldn't understand how people could live like that.

By the time my domesticated son had supplied us all with tea, Gina was back wearing jeans and a T-shirt, with a pair of shabby trainers on her feet in place of the biker's boots.

She sat opposite us and cradled a beaker of tea. "What is it I'm supposed to have done?"

"You handed us a memory stick holding video footage from the CCTV cameras in the ghost train," Mandy declared while Simon made ready to take notes. "When we checked there were twenty minutes of that video missing. Ether the CCTV camera failed or it was deliberately eliminated after it was downloaded from the computer controlling the camera. Which is it?"

I had to hand it to Gina. She posed a model of self-control. "Search me. You think I know anything about that kinda stuff? I just checked it out now and then when the train was running to make sure there were no probs. The first I noticed was when it showed Frank laid under the car. That's when I went in to see what was going on."

Mandy was slightly perplexed and looked as if she was uncertain where to go next, so I stepped in. "Are you saying you had nothing to do with the download?"

"Wouldn't know where to start."

"Then who did?" Mandy demanded, picking up my thread.

"Haven't a clue. Ossie Travis gave me the memory stick, but I don't know that he dealt with the downloading. All he said was he was looking for you guys and he couldn't find you."

"Oh, come on," Simon protested. "We weren't that difficult to pin down."

Gina shrugged again. "Talk to him, not me." She swilled down half the mug of tea. "Is that it. Have you done with me now?"

Simon nodded and Mandy said, "I have no more questions."

"Well, I have," I declared and Gina promptly appealed to the police.

"Do I have to answer her?"

"No," Mandy said, "but if you don't I'll ask the same questions and you'll have to answer me." My friend nodded at me and I took Gina on.

"I was at the shooting gallery. I'd already asked Rachel to come and see me. You were heading for the ticket booth to relieve her. We made eye contact and you changed your mind. I was making my way here and you went riding past on you bike. You were making sure you didn't have to talk to me about Jim Singer's missing gun."

"Because I knew you'd accuse me of taking it."

"And did you?" Mandy wanted to know.

"No, I did not, and I'm sick of seeing her since Thursday." She pointed an accusing finger at me as the 'her' in question.

"I'm doing the job your father paid me to do."

"Yeah, well, like you said, he isn't here anymore. You've been paid, you've been told it had nothing to do with any of us, so get off my back."

"Not while I think you know more than you're telling me or the police." I drank the rest of my tea, got to my feet and prepared to leave. At the door, I turned to stare back at her. "I will be back again, Ms Kilsby."

As always, she didn't look especially interested or impressed.

I stepped out into the heat of afternoon, and strode away, my anger still bubbling away just beneath the surface.

"Chrissy. Hang on. Wait up a minute."

I glance over my shoulder to see Mandy hurrying after me, Simon right behind her.

"I'm carrying two of us, remember." She patted her bump as she caught up to me. "You're taking this too personally."

"I was hired to do a job, Mandy. I didn't do it. I failed. Do you know what that feels like?"

"Of course I do. Do you know how many unsolved crimes we've got on our books?"

"Murders?"

"Well, not murders, no, but we have plenty of assaults and stuff. You did the job for long enough, so you know the score. You're gonna drive yourself up the wall if you don't back off and chill out."

"The sarge is right, Mam," Simon agreed. "Why don't you go and find Dad. We'll talk to Travis."

They were right. I knew they were but this was a matter of personal pride. I had let a client down. The conversation wound down naturally, and I went in search of Dennis. I found him at Sandra's van, and after a few minutes with her, we ambled towards the exit.

"Are you letting it go or what?" he asked as we got near to the ghost train.

"I can't, Dennis. I can't help remembering that man. He came to me for help and I let him down."

"No winning with you, is there? Not unless it's you who's winning anyway." He glanced over to his right. "Tsk. Have you seen the state of that?"

He pointed to a large, white card which Nick had taped to the rope blocking off access to the ghost train.

THIS GOST TRAYNE IS SHUT BY ORDA OF THE PLICE.

My blood ran cold, my heart rate increased and as I scrabbled for my phone, I could barely stop my hands from shaking.

"Mandy. Get down to the ghost train right now. I've got him."

Chapter Nineteen

"If Paddy finds out about this, Chrissy, he'll eat me for lunch and then have my unborn child for afters."

I'd suffered a disturbed night. Nick Kilsby guilty of the murder or manslaughter of his own grandfather? It explained so much about the attitude of both Rachel and Gina. The boy was a simpleton. Unkind but true, and they set out to protect him for the simple reason that they knew it was him.

And yet, I couldn't accept it. He wrote the threatening note to Frank. Of that I was certain. He stole the rifle from Singer. Another sure fire bet. But cutting down the Dracula puppet knowing it would bring Frank there? Hiding in the ghost train tunnel waiting for him? Shooting him so that he would fall across the track and the next car along would kill him? I doubted that Nick had the wit to think up something so complex, never mind carry it out.

By ten o'clock Sunday morning, I could stand it no longer. I had to get to the truth, and there was only one way. I had to speak to the boy.

There was no way Paddy Quinn would let me, but he wouldn't be at Haxford station that early, so I rang Mandy and arranged to meet her there. She took some persuading, but I got my way, and at half past ten, we were ready to see him. He had already been browbeaten by Quinn and a sergeant from Huddersfield, and Quinn had left strict instructions that no one was to question him until he came back on Sunday. At that point, Mandy made the comment about Quinn's reaction to our speaking with Nick.

"And what about innocence, Mandy? Doesn't it matter than Nick is not guilty?" I piled the pressure on. "Besides, if you don't let me speak to him, I'll talk to my brother, get him appointed as Nick's solicitor, and he'll ask the questions I need answers to."

A conditional surrender from Mandy. "Just keep it quiet. I'll make sure Hillman doesn't add your name to the interview list."

"Tell him if he dares I'll make sure everyone in Haxford knows his nickname is Minx."

As it turned out, it wasn't a problem. Rehana Suleman was on duty and she was an old friend. When Mandy told her it was an informal chat with Nick and she didn't want my name mentioned, Rehana agreed right away, and she did so with a conspiratorial smirk on her angelic face.

Nick looked a sorry sight when we sat with him. He'd obviously been crying and he was shaking as if frightened that we were going to attack him.

I made an effort to reassure him. "Hello, Nick. You do know who I am, don't you?"

"You're that Mrs nosy woman who's been asking all them questions. You were talking to me yesterday."

"I am and I was." I thought it easier to agree with him rather than correct him on my name and purpose. "But you can call me Christine." I delivered the invitation with a friendly smile. "Are they treating you all right?"

"They're accusing me of stuff I haven't done."

"I know that, and we're going to try persuading Mr Quinn that you didn't do it. But you did write that note, to your granddad, didn't you?"

His shoulders dropped and his head bowed. "Yes." He said it in such a tiny, distant voice that I knew he was not only afraid but ashamed.

"Why did you send it?"

He looked up and amongst the flow of tears I could see and hear the anger. "Cos of what he did to my mam."

This was a new angle. Had Frank Kilsby been beating his daughter?

"What did he do, Nick? What did he do to Gina?"

"Me." He turned a furious forefinger into his chest. "He weren't just me granddad, you know."

With those few words, the full horror of Frank Kilsby sank in and sparked my fury. If he had been standing there in front of me, I would have needed no air rifle, no random car on a ghost train track. I would have beaten him to death with my bare hands. The level of disgust and contempt I felt for him made me want to scream and vomit.

I was unable to say it, but Mandy had no such problem.

"He was your father too?" When Nick nodded, she went on, "He raped your mother, his own daughter?"

Once again Nick replied with a mute nod, and if

he really had killed Frank, I could have understood, but I knew he hadn't. This poor young man did not have the brains to plan such a killing.

"How did you find out, Nick?" I asked.

"Me gran told me."

That was a puzzle. Nick's grandmother would have been Kilsby's first wife, but according to Rachel, she left years before the boy was born.

"Your gran... Oh. You mean Rachel?"

He nodded again.

Mandy took the lead. "Right, so you sent him the note. How did you intend making sure he would be killed?"

"I didn't kill him but I was gonna. I cut part through the rope on the slingshot. See, sometimes, when we set up, he'd try the slingshot, and I was gonna push him into trying it out. Call him out as a coward if he didn't. He'd go for it just to prove he had the bottle. And then when the rope snapped, the carriage would crash and he'd get his."

"But Ossie checked it before it was set up," I said, "and he insisted Frank replace it. What did you do then, Nick?"

"Nothing. I was trying to think of some other way of getting him and the only thing I could think was to shoot him, so I pinched one of Jim Singer's guns that night while everyone was asleep, but I didn't know they wouldn't fire real bullets."

"What did you do with the rifle?" Mandy asked.

"I hid it under that fat woman's snack bar, that Sandra. I reckon it's still there."

Another little mystery cleared up. "Let's go back to the note," I suggested. "You wrote about

Walpurgis. Do you know what it is?"

"I heard Márta talking about it. I didn't know we were getting a Walpurgis, but I couldn't wait to see it."

More mystification. "Nick, are you sure you know what Walpurgis means?"

"Course I do. I've seen 'em on the telly. Big fat things, like whales, only they have these great big teeth. Husks I think they're called."

"Tusks not husks, and that's a walrus," I said, and turned to Mandy. "This has been a humungous catalogue of errors from minute one. This boy's no more guilty than I am."

"I'm beginning to think you're right." She concentrated on him. "Tell us about the morning Frank was killed, Nick. What were you doing?"

"I told that other bloke. Mr Quinn. I were working the ghost train station. Mam was at the control box, and I were letting the punters in and out of the cars. I never moved. Not even when Mam went in to see what had happened to granddad... dad."

"So you don't know who fooled around with the Dracula puppet?"

He shrugged. "Coulda bin anybody. Ossie were in there earlier, checking everything was all right, but he didn't say nothing about the puppet being loose."

Right then I began to see what this was about. "You saw him go in?"

He nodded. "I had to go for a wee, and as I cut round the back I saw him going in."

That was all I needed. With that tiny snippet of

information, I knew who was responsible but more than that, I knew why. "Mandy, you should let this boy go, and lets you and me get out to the fair. I know everything now."

"Based on his say so?" She pointed at Nick. "Anyway, he might still face charges over the gun and the note."

"Chickenfeed. He did nothing with them and you can let him off with a caution."

"Chrissy, if Ossie hadn't checked that bungee rope, Kilsby would be dead."

"He is dead in case you've forgotten, and I think that bungee rope is what gave our man the idea."

Mandy was obviously puzzled by this but she acquiesced and leaving Rehana to escort Nick back to his cell, we hurried out of the station, pausing only to order support at the fair, jumped into her car and with all lights, emergency and otherwise blazing, and sirens screaming at the traffic, we tore off towards Barncroft's Meadow.

"Come on, Chrissy. Tell me what's been going on or what you think's been going on?"

"A huge insurance scam. Ossie told me a few days ago that Kilsby was well-insured, but it was attached to the bank loans financing the fair. Remember that Ossie is smarter than your average fairground worker. Ex-college boy. Not only that, he was sleeping with Rachel. I'm guessing he checked the insurance policies, although he denied it, learned that aside from those covering the loans, Kilsby had other policies worth quite a bit of money. Maybe I'm wrong. Maybe he had a buyer standing by to take the fair over. Somewhere along the line he and Rachel stood to make a lot of money, but only when Frank died. So they decided that Haxford Wool Fair was the perfect venue to be rid of him. Small Yorkshire town, small police force. But first they needed a scapegoat and they chose Nick."

"Not too strong in the brain department."

"Exactly. Tell him that Kilsby raped his mother and he was the result, and it would drive the kid mad. Not so much his parentage, but the rape. Say what you like, but that boy loves his mother."

As we cut off onto Derbyshire Road, Mandy expressed her doubts. "It all sounds a bit complicated to me, Chrissy. I mean, let's say Ossie saw the kid cutting the bungee rope. If he wanted Frank out of the way, why didn't he just leave it? Let the slingshot do the job for him?"

"Because there always the danger that Frank wouldn't ride the slingshot and it would kill a customer and that could have been a total disaster, not only for Kilsby, but Ossie too. Ossie was the technical expert, remember."

"Point taken, but I still think it's too complicated."

As we turned into the fair, the car park attendant got out of the way sharp and I gave him a smile and wave as we passed. Mandy took it steady, weaving through the growing Sunday crowds until we got to the accommodation zone, where we found Ossie sitting on the step outside Rachel's van, stroking Kaiser's ear.

"Its Mrs Giddy-one of the Yard and Miss Marbles." He smiled at us. "I've been expecting you ever since that idiot boss of yours arrested Nick earlier. In fact, if you hadn't turned up by lunchtime I was going to come to the station to sort it out." He got to his feet. "Nick didn't kill Kilsby. Or more accurately, Nick didn't shoot him to make him fall. I did. But it was an accident."

"We know." I said. "Well, we know you shot him."

"Come in. Let's have a cuppa."

"You're under arrest, Mr Travis," Mandy insisted.

"Sure. I know you have your job to do, but I'm not going anywhere, so let me tell you what happened before you cuff me."

Without waiting for us, he disappeared to the van and we followed, only to find him stood by the table with an automatic pistol in his hand.

Mandy and I were on immediate alert and I made an effort to dissuade him. "Please don't do it, Ossie. We've got a swarm of uniforms outside. You won't get away with it. And besides, Mandy's pregnant."

It was as if he'd just noticed the gun. "What? Oh, sorry." He spun it expertly in his hand and offered it to Mandy, butt first. "It's a BB pistol. The one that shot Frank and knocked him out. I've had it for years and I didn't even realise it had any pellets in it. I only meant to threaten him with it and even that was in the heat of the moment."

Mandy slipped on a pair of forensic gloves and took the gun, dropping it into an evidence bag.

Ossie made his way to the kettle and we sat down blocking his exit. A quick glance through the windows revealed half a dozen uniforms guarding any possible attempt at escape.

"You disgust me," I told him when he delivered tea. "All this just for money?"

He was as laid back as ever. "What are you talking about, Christine?"

"We know it all," Mandy said, and proceeded to explain my earlier deductions. He listened without interrupting and when she'd finished, he burst out laughing.

"I've never heard so much twaddle in my life."

I could feel my ears colouring. Had I got it wrong? Impossible. "Suppose you give us your version."

"Well, to begin with, Rache didn't tell Nick that Frank was his father. He overheard an argument between Rache and Frank, during which Rache accused him of raping Gina when she was just a kid. I knew what it would do to Nick, so I kept an eye on him. I saw him cut the slingshot rope, and covered for him. But at the same time, I had a word with Gina, and you can ask her if you don't believe me. Yes, Frank did abuse her when she was a teenager, but she insists that Frank is not Nick's father. She won't say who it is because she was under age and she doesn't want to get the father into trouble. If you want my biased opinion, I reckon it's Eddie Zannis. He and Gina have been an item on and off for years, but I wouldn't bet on her backing up any attempt to prosecute him."

I ignored his opinions on Nick's parentage. "Did you know that Nick stole the rifle from Jim Singer?" I was still annoyed that he was trying to blow my fanciful theory apart.

"No, but I figured he'd try again, so I decided to intervene. To be honest when I learned that Frank really had abused Gina, I was steaming angry. She might not be a relative, but I like that girl. She's tough, independent, a good kid at heart, and she's always taken care of Nick. Didn't I tell you she made an effort to educate him? All right, so she failed, but she didn't deserve that kind of treatment from her father. Anyway, I was with Frank when Gina called him for the Dracula puppet. Frank went in the front way and I went in through the back. We were arguing the toss and hiding when the cars came through. I told him exactly what I thought of him and he sacked me on the spot. I took the pistol out and told him, someone should blow his rotten head off. He said go ahead. I ducked the issue, he grabbed the pistol and my finger caught the trigger." Ossie shrugged. "I told you. I didn't realise it was loaded. He didn't go down but he was staggering. He told me that was it, I was fired, get out of his sight, so I just walked off and left him to it. If I'd known he would fall across the tracks, I'd have waited and helped him, but I was so mad that it didn't occur to me. I just stormed away."

It sounded acceptable, but there was a snag. Two, actually. "How did you get in and out through the back door without anyone detecting daylight coming through when you opened that rear door?"

He chuckled and drank off half his beaker of tea. "If we set the slingshot up as efficiently as you people do your homework, we'd have bodies all over the place. Not one of you has ever checked that back access, have you? When you open it, you're in a cubby hole. You close the outer door and then let yourself in through the second door. It's in a spot where the nearest cars are moving away from you, and the next car hasn't come to the final bend."

That annoyed me even further. "It doesn't show on the plan you gave me."

There was that insouciant smile again. "A spot of editing before I handed it over. Sorry, Christine."

And so to the second outstanding problem. "Who cut Frank's brakes outside the Haxford Arms?" I demanded.

He shrugged. "I really don't know."

"I'll bet there's a steak knife missing from Gina's cutlery drawer."

"Even if there is, can you prove it was Nick?"

***

He had to be arrested and charged, and Paddy Quinn, who was busy interrogating Nick again, went ballistic when Mandy got back to the station with Ossie.

Ossie made a free statement admitting to everything, leaving Nick to face some lesser charges. After formally charging Ossie with manslaughter, even though there was no guarantee that it would stand up in court, Paddy went back to Huddersfield in a huge sulk, leaving Mandy to handle Nick.

When questioned again, he denied cutting Frank's brake lines, but I suspected it was him. Perhaps the boy wasn't quite as gormless as people assumed.

Mandy wasn't sure what charges she could bring

other than malicious damage to the slingshot, the theft of a BB rifle, which he promised to return, and sending a mischievous, badly spelled communication. After consulting her station commander, she gave the boy a written caution.

I drove him back to Barncroft's Meadow after she released him, and escorted him to his mother's van where Gina listened to his tale, and promised to sit him down and talk to him about his antecedents.

When I left, she escorted me back to my car. "I didn't trust you," she said as I unlocked the doors. "We're like that, fairground folk. We don't trust townies like you. But I've been sick with worry ever since that detective took Nick in. You got him off though, so it's one I owe you."

"Your father paid me to get to the bottom of the mystery, Gina, and that's exactly what I did. I'm glad I could help."

"What'll happen to Ossie?"

I shrugged. "He'll be charged and he could go to prison. But there's no one to argue with his account of events, unless you've got it on CCTV somewhere."

"I have, and he's telling the truth."

"So it really was you who cut that footage from the CCTV camera?"

She nodded. "I had to. We could have sorted it ourselves."

"And now that it might help keep him out of jail, what will you do?"

She shrugged this time. "If I take it to them, they'll book me for withholding evidence, won't they?"

"They might. Then again, if you could persuade them that it's only just turned up on the laptop, they might not."

She laughed. I'm sure it was the first time I'd seen her break a smile. "I'll think about it."

Epilogue

Oswald Travis was charged with involuntary manslaughter at tried at Leeds Crown Court.

During his trial, he also took responsibility for cutting out the missing section of video and admitted to cutting Kilsby's brake lines while the truck was parked at the Haxford Arms, this despite the fact that he denied it when he spoke to Mandy and me. Privately, I was sure he didn't do it. I think it was Nick, but I elected to keep my mouth shut.

The court took account of his agitated state at the time, and of Frank Kilsby's appalling behaviour, but the judge could not overlook that Ossie was carrying a firearm in the shape of the air pistol. He was sentenced to six years in prison. On reflection, considering the charges to which he confessed, he was lucky to get away with such a light sentence.

Haxford Wool Fair reached its end on the first bank holiday in May, and two days later, Ketchak's Funfair trundled out of the town on its way to pastures new. A phone call from Gina on the day they left told me that Frank's insurers would settle the outstanding loans, and Rachel swore that no matter how long he served in prison, she would wait for Ossie.

Banjo the bun thief turned out for a couple more

shows and as George Ibble predicted, he didn't even earn a place, but he's a young dog yet. He has time to learn.

And me? I learned a couple of valuable lessons during those few days, the most important of which was KISS – Keep It Simple, Stupid, where stupid is me. I made too many mistakes in that investigation, missed too many connections, and even Dennis had to put me right… although as it turned out, he was as wrong as everyone else about that rear door showing daylight.

They were mistakes, I promised myself, I wouldn't make again.

And that concludes this edition of Christine Capper's Comings & Goings. Tune in again next week when I'll have more tales from the heart of Haxford.

THE END

The Author

David W Robinson retired from the rat race after the other rats objected to his participation, and he now lives with his long-suffering wife in sight of the Pennine Moors outside Manchester.

Best known as the creator of the light-hearted **Sanford 3rd Age Club Mysteries**, and in the same vein, the brand new series, **Mrs Capper's Casebook**. He also produces darker, more psychological crime thrillers; the **Feyer & Drake** thrillers and occasional standalone titles.

He, produces his own videos, and can frequently be heard grumbling against the world on Facebook at **https://www.facebook.com/dwrobinson3** and has a YouTube channel at **https://www.youtube.com/user/Dwrob96/videos**. For more information you can track him down at **www.dwrob.com**

By the same author

(All titles are exclusive to Amazon)

Self-Published works

Mrs Capper's Casebooks
Mrs Capper's Christmas
Death at the Wool Fair
Blackmail at the Ballot Box
A Professional Dilemma

Titles published and managed by Darkstroke Books

The Sanford 3rd Age Club Mysteries
The Filey Connection
The I-spy Murders
A Halloween Homicide
A Murder for Christmas
Murder at the Murder Mystery Weekend
My Deadly Valentine
The Chocolate Egg Murders
The Summer Wedding Murder
Costa del Murder
Christmas Crackers
Death in Distribution
A Killing in the Family
A Theatrical Murder
Trial by Fire
Peril in Palmanova
The Squires Lodge Murders
Murder at the Treasure Hunt
A Cornish Killing

Merry Murders Everyone
Tales from the Lazy Luncheonette Casebook
A Tangle in Tenerife
Tis the Season to Be Murdered
Confusion in Cleethorpes
Murder on the Movie Set
A Deadly Twixmas
Naked Murder

The Midthorpe Mysteries
Missing on Midthorpe
Bloodshed in Benidorm

Feyer & Drake
The Anagramist
The Frame

Standalone titles
The Cutter
Kracht

THANK YOU FOR READING. I HOPE YOU HAVE ENJOYED THIS BOOK. IF SO IT WOULD BE WONDERFUL IF YOU COULD LEAVE A REVIEW ON AMAZON?